Y ou're not our dog, the part stings. Of cou I'm their dog.

If I go with them, the credits that I've earned toward being a therapy dog. I am four visits away, three if this meeting counts. A whisker away. *Almost.*

Will they still let me be a therapy dog if I go?

Will they let me be one if I *don't*?

I try to remember if we covered runaway clients in my training. My instinct tells me: I can't let them just wander away. These clients, these humans—I love them. They are my pack. My duty. They are still full of holes that haven't yet been filled, and my job is to fill them. To guide them. My job is to be their moon.

Also by Kristin O'Donnell Tubb
A Dog Like Daisy
Zeus, Dog of Chaos

KRISTIN O'DONNELL TUBB

LUNA

HOWLS AT THE MOON

KATHERINE TEGEN BOOKS
An Imprint of HarperCollins Publishers

Katherine Tegen Books is an imprint of HarperCollins Publishers.

Luna Howls at the Moon

Library of Congress Control Number: 2020952902
ISBN 978-0-06-301863-1

Typography by Andrea Vandergrift
22 23 24 25 26   PC/BRR   10 9 8 7 6 5 4 3 2 1
❖
First paperback edition, 2022

For Sandi
and for those who are growing
through therapy and counseling

★ 1 ★

NOT ALMOST

Most of my clients don't mind when I lick their tears away. Others want me to roll over and show them my belly. Still others just want the big, soft, blinky eyes coupled with a slow wag. Or a goofy jangle of my tags. Or letting my tongue loll out. Sometimes I chase my tail, even though it makes me dizzy and I know I'm never going to catch that rascal. But I do it because it makes the client happy. It's all about the client. Reading them and responding. Making them feel safe. Secure. Confident. Each of us has a different hole that needs filling. My job as a therapy dog is to find the shape of that hole and fill it. That's why my name is Luna. Just like the moon, I change shape. I become what others need to see.

It works like . . . a yawn. *Yaaaawwwwwn.* When someone yawns, others yawn. It's catching, but in a subtle, gentle way. That's how it feels to pick up on others' emotions.

A yawn? My classmate Goliath scoffs when I ask him if that's how the job works for him too. *Hey, fellas! Luna here says her job is a big yawn. Maybe you need a new line of work, kid. Something more exciting— a rodeo dog, maybe? The circus?*

All the other dogs huddled in this too-bright church basement wag their tails, rattle their tags, sneeze. They laugh, but the emotion around their chuckles isn't joy. It feels sharper, darker; honed to pierce like a thorn.

My instinct is to be upset, but duty says I should remain calm. I often have to defy my instincts because my training says that I should be both calm and calming. Duty over instinct, always. So I laugh too, because I don't want the others at Therapy Dogs Worldwide to think I'm weird or different or something.

The only dog who doesn't laugh is Samwise. Samwise has her 400-visit pin. That makes her a Distinguished Therapy Dog by TDW standards, and that's all you need to know about Samwise. Impressive.

Seriously, though, Luna. Take it from me. Goliath

twitches and scratches his perky chihuahua ear. He's the itchiest dog I've ever met. *You get too close*, Goliath says. *You FEEL too much. All your clients want? To give you a pat here, a hug there. That's it. You don't owe them anything more than that. You need to grow thicker fur, kid.*

I hate it when Goliath calls me kid, because we're the same age. That, and I'm about four times his size. I'm a silver Labrador, but Goliath makes me feel like a rusty mutt. We went through class together at Therapy Dogs Worldwide. Just because he earned his 50-visit pin faster than any other dog in our class—faster than any other dog in TDW history—he thinks his breath doesn't stink. His head's gotten so big I don't know how they get his leash on.

The light in this stuffy room shifts, and I feel sudden smiles in the air. "Okay, everyone," says Barb, the leader of the local TDW chapter. I love her, so I let her know with a tail wag. "The photographer here wants to get several shots for the *American-Statesman*. All of Austin will read about what good dogs you are!"

Good dogs. We wag. The joy caused by eight dogs all wagging tails together feels like a perfect slant of sunshine.

"Okay, so, Roy," Barb says, turning to the photographer. "We're here tonight celebrating the dogs who just got their fifty-visit pin. Once the dogs have made fifty different visits to clients, they become official TDW therapy dogs, and we reward their hard work with one of these." Barb holds up a small blue pin, and rays of light ping off it. It shines like a tiny star. It's more beautiful than greasy sausage.

"That'll be yours soon, Luna," Tessa whispers to me. Tessa. She's my human. Well, I have lots of humans in my line of work, but she's the main one. Tessa makes me imagine a honeybee: hardworking, always thinking of her hive. She rubs my soft ear and it feels so good my back leg thumps *thank you thank you thank you.*

"So let's start with a photo of all the dogs who have their fifty-visit pin, then," the photographer, Roy, says. He waves his camera at a colorful sign. "Stand around that banner."

Every dog in the room moves toward the sign. Every dog but me. The air in this creepy-drippy basement darkens, and I feel like that perfect slant of sun has disappeared behind a cloud. I sulk.

"Cheese!" the humans all shout, and I drool like I do every time humans take photos, because why do they always shout that?! Roy's camera pops like fire-crackers. He shifts his camera sideways and takes more photos. He changes positions and takes more photos. He stands on a chair and takes more photos.

Alone I sit. I sulk harder. The air gets heavier. *Grow thicker fur*, Goliath said. How would that help? Every strand of my fur feels like a tiny rag, soaking up all the moods around me. How would having *more* fur help? What's wrong with me that I *feel* so much? All the time?

"So why aren't they wearing vests?" Roy asks, waving the lens of his camera over the gang of dogs between clicks. "They're service dogs, right?"

Barb smiles. "I'm glad you asked that, Roy. No, they aren't service dogs. They're therapy dogs. A bit like emotional support dogs, but they comfort many people, not just one. Some of these dogs visit hospitals, some visit retirement centers. Some are placed in schools and libraries to help with reading programs. Some work with therapists and counselors as they meet with their clients. But therapy dogs wear bandannas instead of vests because they are meant to be hugged and petted as often as possible. These dogs are *heroes*."

That's what I want to be too. A *hero*. And I'm almost there. When I get that pin, everyone will know it. They will know I put duty first. I think of that shiny pin and I can't help but wag. And so, the air shifts again. Shimmery this time, like starlight poking holes in the dark. I smile and my tongue lolls out of my mouth. I will be a star.

Barb looks over at Tessa and me, standing on the opposite side of the room, alone. Her face changes, and I feel her *pity*. *Pity* feels green and tight and sour like wild apples.

"Oh, can we get one more photo with Luna in it?" Barb asks. "She's only nine visits away from her fifty-visit pin. Such a good girl."

I love Barb. I tell her this again with my tail. I stand, ready to be photographed and famous.

"Can't," Roy says, slamming his camera equipment into multiple bags and zipping them shut. "Gotta go shoot the school board meeting next."

Goliath snickers loudly, and the others follow suit. *So close there, Luna. SO CLOSE. You sure seem to live a life of almosts.*

What a bunch of thorns.

As if she hears them, my honeybee Tessa scratches my neck. "Nine visits, girl. Almost there. The next party will be for you."

Nine visits. Nine more client visits and I'll get my own tiny star pinned to my bandanna. The tiny star that will let everyone know I'm not weird or different or something. That I take my duty seriously. That I'm not *almost*.

★ 2 ★

UNCERTAINTY IS LIKE
DRINKING MUDDY WATER

Who's ready to go to work?" Tessa asks, and I bark and wag and spinspinspin as a reply. Tessa knots my bandanna around my neck. It's crisp and red and it smells like months of comforting kid humans. Like laughter and tears and hugs and sighs.

I love the routine Tessa and I have. I study feelings. I try to define emotions. I don't understand them all, and sometimes they overwhelm me. That's when I remember my duty: calm and calming. But the routine is nice: wake, eat, work, sleep. Quiet habits fill our days.

Tessa tugs the bandanna around my neck and gives me a delicious scratch. We feel excited and a bit nervous today, it seems; it feels like the thrill of riding in a car with the windows down, all bugs and wind and sun, but the road is curvy and bumpy.

We are trying something *new*.

"This group session will be good," Tessa says, running her fingers over my sleek ears. But it sounds like she's saying this to herself rather than to me. Humans do that a lot to dogs: tell them things they need to hear themselves. Things like *she's a good girl* and *I love you*. Tessa continues, "I've decided we're going to focus on managing emotions in this group. My mentor says group sessions can sometimes get out of hand, but I don't think we need to worry about that with these kids. We know these kids, don't we, Luna? They're great. It'll be great."

This group thing: it's not our regular routine. It's new. New feels *uncertain*, like drinking muddy water. You're never quite sure what you're getting from a mud puddle. But I trust Tessa. And I trust these clients of ours.

It is the orange part of the day, and sun paints everything the color of poppies. Tessa lifts a plastic tub full of art supplies out of the back of her car and settles it on her hip. But instead of us going to our cozy trailer in the church parking lot like we usually do, she uses a key to unlock the door down to the church basement. The same basement where I didn't become famous because they didn't take my picture for the paper. *Almost.*

I don't like this place. I pause going down the narrow wooden steps.

Tessa must sense my hesitation, because she smiles her sunflower smile, the one that turns people toward her. "We have to meet as a group down here, Luna. Not enough room in our trailer. We can be brave."

It's not a question, and I love that about Tessa. She knows when to ask for bravery, and when to announce it's needed.

I totter down the stairs and into the drippy, weird basement. The lights flicker on in sections like lightning. I hear a toilet running, so I seek it out down a dark hallway and take huge gulps of cold water before we start our day. *Whew.* Much better. There's nothing in the world a little toilet water can't fix.

When I return, Tessa has spilled colorful art supplies all over the tabletops, and my tail wags because ART! Art smells like glue and paint and crayons and oils and it makes humans feel hummy happy, like shimmery, buzzing birds sipping sugar water.

Anticipation is like hearing the word *walk*, seeing the leash, but then not leaving right away. It's what I feel now. I wait for my clients to arrive. Should I sit? No, too casual. Stand? Too formal. I pace, because I'm uncertain what to expect with all my clients here in one room, together. Tessa feels the same. She chews on a piece of rubber, blows a bubble, and *pop*! Cracks it against her lips.

Caleb arrives first. My ears perk toward him. "Where's the chessboard?"

Tessa smiles. "I have it, but I thought we might start with some art first."

Caleb feels as hesitant as a dog on a too-short leash. My whiskers twitter. But he enters and picks a seat in front of a rainbow of oil paints. His knee bounces beneath the table and the paints dance across the table-top before he realizes that his long, lanky legs are the ones making them hop.

Without asking Tessa, Caleb leaps up, takes one of the bowls of water that are supposed to be for art, and places it near my paws. He doesn't say anything, doesn't even meet my eyes, but he seems to know I was thirsty earlier. I thank him with my tail. He drops back into his chair and his knees bounce more.

Amelia and Hector arrive at the same moment. My nostrils twitch between the two of them, trying to untangle the air around them so I can sense each one. Amelia hugs me quickly (she smells like grass) and then glides to the paints too. Hector bumps down the stairs with his bike over his shoulder, then chooses a spot far down the table, next to a pile of wrinkly magazines and a snarl of scissors.

Waterfall. Rock. Shadow. That's what these three are.

I feel the Knot approach before she even enters. She bang bang bangs down the basement steps in her tooth-boots and falls into a metal chair that groans in reply. "Sorry I'm late."

Beatrice the Knot sits in front of a huge lump of clay. Her jeans are worn and spattered with paint, almost as if she got a head start on arting.

Tessa talks about groups and growth, and I stand nearby and *sniiiiiiffff*. Twitch my whiskers. Adjust my ears. It's odd, all these feelings together, like trying to sort through the smells wafting off a lovely garbage can.

And then they *create*. Art makes humans see things the same way the artist sees them, and it makes humans see things differently than they have before. Both same and different. And creating art makes human feelings smooth out, brighten, clarify, like a sheen of ice over a nighttime pond.

When the Knot and the Shadow, the Waterfall and the Rock start arting, they focus. They stick tongues out of the corners of their mouths. They sit less erect. They breathe evenly.

It's working! I wag at Tessa. These clients are loosening, lightening.

11

Beatrice moves from massaging a lump of clay to pounding it. She stands to pound better, *pound pound pound*. She doesn't seem to notice the glare that Caleb shoots her as the paints leap around the table. Amelia grins down at her piece of paper and keeps swooshing colors across it like comets. Hector cuts apart panels of a comic strip from a newspaper, *snip snip snip*.

Beatrice pounds more, lifts her chin at Hector's comic. "You know, at my school they won't let us read graphic novels for book reports? Isn't that the stupidest thing you've ever heard?"

Pound pound pound. Snip snip snip. The room is silent.

Caleb bites his bottom lip. We feel *undecided*, I realize. But he says it anyway: "Probably not THE stupidest, but yes. Pretty ridiculous."

Beatrice pauses the pounding. I can't get a read on her feelings because we're swirling through so many so quickly. "You like graphic novels?"

Caleb nods once. "I do."

"Which ones?" The way Beatrice says it, it sounds more like blame than a question.

"*Bone. Amulet.* And I read lots of comics."

"Marvel or DC?"

"Marvel, of course."

Beatrice smirks, and if I were human, I might be

confused by that. But I know by her scent that she's satisfied with that answer. *This is working!* I wag more.

Pound pound pound. Snip snip snip. The room is silent again.

"You could start a petition, you know." Caleb bites his lip again, dabs his paintbrush in gray paint. He is painting a chessboard, I see.

"A what?" *Pound pound pound.*

"A petition. It's a formally written request. A document that—"

"I *know* what a petition *is*!" Beatrice cocks her head at Caleb, and the bun on top of her head slides around like a tennis ball. I copy her; I cock my head too. Always let the client take the lead. Duty first. "I just didn't know what you meant by that."

"You could draw up a petition to change that rule about graphic novels. Write something up on your computer. Get all your friends to sign it. Give it to the administrators. Maybe they'd change that rule." Caleb says all of this without once looking up from the gray-and-white chessboard he's painting.

Beatrice narrows her eyes at him. I narrow my eyes too. Our lips flatten. "You don't know if that would work," she says.

"I do know."

It is quiet, so he continues. "At my school there was

13

this form we all had to fill out. And on it, you had to pick your race. White, African American, Native American, Asian American . . . you know. But checking *white* felt like I was choosing my dad's family over my mom's and checking *Black* felt like I was choosing Mom's family over Dad's. You'd think they'd have a box that said *Multiracial*, but they didn't. I knew they wanted me to check *Other*, you know? But I didn't like that term. *Other*. So I started a petition where we could check more than one box."

It is the most I've ever heard Caleb talk. He dips his paintbrush in gray paint again. It is still quiet, but Beatrice wears a small grin. Amelia nods. Hector stops snipping.

"And I won," Caleb tells his chessboard. "Now I check more than one box."

Beatrice nods. Knocks the table. This story *satisfies* her, like a nice steak taco. "More than one box. Dude. I get that."

They continue to art.

Pound pound pound. Snip snip snip.

Beatrice leans over Amelia's painting. "Wow! Wouldja look at that!"

Amelia burns like she's had too much sun on her skin, but she beams.

14

"Is that a bomb?" Beatrice says, pointing at Amelia's paper. Amelia nods.

Tessa scoots over there, and I feel her have a flutter of panic at this. "A bomb?" She leans over the painting. Her heart calms and she says, "Oh! It's exploding with flowers! How lovely, Amelia."

"My grammy used to say this thing," Beatrice says quietly. "She always said she wasn't fragile like a flower; she was fragile like a *bomb*."

Beatrice clears her throat and tries to hide the sudden shine that's appeared on her eyes. The word *grammy* always makes Bea choke up. She hooks her thumbs in the loops on her paint-spattered jeans and bounces on her toes. Amelia smiles large, larger, and nods.

Tessa's eyes widen. "Amelia! I'm so glad to see you using your nonverbal language with Beatrice!"

Tessa no sooner finishes horking up those words than she wishes she could lap them back up again, like vomit. Amelia's face lines slant down sharply, and instead of now burning like sun on skin, she burns like a match. Bea and Caleb seem to sizzle too, but I don't know why. Are they burning because Amelia is? Is it contagious? Amelia crosses her arms and leans back in her chair.

Pound pound pound. Snip snip snip.

"I made a hoverboard with my DI team," Hector says from the end of the table. He doesn't look up from cutting pages of a magazine.

Hector isn't usually one to mind silence, so it surprises me when he talks. I smile, wag my tail slowly to encourage him.

"You mean one of those things you stand on? With two wheels?" Beatrice says. She crosses her arms. She feels *doubt*. I can tell by the way her face pulls to one side. "What's DI?"

"No, those are scooters. True hoverboards don't touch the ground. They hover. Like the name says. And I made one. Destination Imagination." Hector cuts small squares of magazine print the whole time he provides this information.

Beatrice circles the table. Stands over him. "Whoa. Wait. You made a thing that hovers? How?"

"With plywood and a leaf blower and a tarp. And twenty-six other components."

Beatrice turns her head side to side, and her neck goes *Pop! Pop!* "And you can ride it."

"If you don't weigh over a hundred twenty-five pounds, yes."

Beatrice is shaking her head *no* but her face is excited like a *yes*. "Ms. Tessa, did you hear that?"

Tessa smiles. "I did. Hector is very talented in science."

Beatrice is still shaking her head *no*. "I don't believe it floats. I need to see this thing."

Hector isn't mad at Beatrice's *no* head. "It floats. And you can ride it. If you don't weigh more than a hundred twenty-five pounds."

Beatrice leaps toward Tessa. "Ms. Tessa, can he bring it next time?" Beatrice sweeps her hand across the church basement. "There's plenty of room in here for us to try this thing. I need to see if it works."

Tessa twirls a lock of her hair, which is her sign for *I want to say no but I need to figure out how to say no gently.*

"I can bring it," Hector says. "It works. And you can ride it." Hector looks up for the first time at Beatrice, scanning her quickly. "If you don't weigh more than a hundred twenty-five pounds."

Tessa is really tugging on her hair now. "Bring a helmet too, Hector."

He nods once. "I always bring a helmet."

Silence again.

Pound pound pound. Snip snip snip.

Caleb stands to look at his chessboard from a taller angle. I do envy that humans can perch on back legs and see farther. It must hurt, though, balancing like that all the time.

Caleb dips his paintbrush into a deep red, and then begins flinging the paint across the precise board he's painted. It looks blood-spattered.

Pound pound pound. Snip snip snip. Fling fling fling.

The rhythm of art is a steady heartbeat.

"Hey, watch it!" Beatrice shouts suddenly, backing away from the table with a loud chair screech. She looks down at her clothes. Circles the table to Caleb's side. "You're getting paint all over me!"

Caleb looks up from his painting. "I don't think so."

The stare between them is like a tug-of-war rope pulled taut. I cross to stand between them. The air feels electric.

Duty first. But whose duty is most important when we're all together in a pack like this?

Beatrice points to paint on her jeans. "Yeah, you did."

Caleb's brow wrinkles like an abandoned blanket. "Your jeans already have paint all over them."

"That's *artistic* paint! Yours is just a mess!"

Caleb blinks. Beatrice cracks her knuckles. Tessa clears her throat. "This looks like a good place to practice some of our conflict resolution techniques." Tessa is trying to stand between them too. "Caleb?"

Caleb circles around to Beatrice's side of the table. "Can I look at the . . . clay you've been punching?"

Beatrice's face falls flat, so mine does too. "It's a pinch pot. You pound it, then you pinch it into a pot shape."

Caleb's hand reaches, reaches toward the lump of clay that Beatrice has been working. I feel the knot inside Beatrice tighten. "Don't touch it!"

But Caleb is a waterfall, rushing water, and sometimes he has a hard time controlling where his path might go. He reaches out and pinches the edge of Beatrice's pot.

"NO!" Beatrice screams. She pounds her fists on the tabletop, and a green bottle of paint topples onto Amelia's painting. Amelia tries to pick her painting up out of the puddle of green but it's too thick. It's too late. Beatrice's knot yanks tighter. "Tessa, I told him no!"

"I'm—I'm sorry," Caleb stammers. He looks down at his own fingers that seemed to betray him, and he wipes clay on the hem of his shirt. Then he swipes a paper towel across the clay now on the hem. "I just wanted to make it up to you. . . ."

Beatrice huffs. Knotted fists rest on her hips. "Tessa, are we done?"

Tessa is chasing her tail here. She knows that this is

the group's first meeting, so she doesn't want to push them too far too fast. But she doesn't want to end the session like this.

"Let's everyone take three deep breaths, and then we'll call it a day." Tessa leads them: Inhale, exhale. Inhale, exhale. Inhale, exhale.

It slows the rush of water, loosens the tight knot. Beatrice says a hasty goodbye and leaves. Caleb picks up his blood-spattered chessboard and gives it to Tessa. Amelia looks at her ruined painting and leaves it soaking in green before slipping away.

And Hector cuts. *Snip snip snip.*

★ 3 ★

BEATRICE THE KNOT

Tessa and I enter one of the trailers behind the church where we work. It's shaky and squeaky and it smells like burnt coffee and old carpet. This trailer is always too cold or too hot, but this is where we *help*. Tessa has lined the homemade bookshelves with games and toys and art supplies. She has cards and balls and sand trays for play therapy. She's hung her granny's old lace curtains in the windows, and she opens them wide or closes them tight, depending on who her client is, on how much light they need. Tessa is good at her job.

First up today: Beatrice. It has been three rainbow days since all my clients met as a group, and Tessa is *anxious* to hear Beatrice's thoughts.

21

Beatrice makes me imagine a knotted rope. A knot ties my bandanna on and can be very useful. But a knot isn't useful when it's just a knot. A tangle. A hiccup in an otherwise smooth rope. They need a purpose, knots. Beatrice thinks the world is filled with tangleless rope. That's why I'm here with her. My duty. I help her see the usefulness of a knot. I help her see we all have tangles.

Tessa flings her granny's lace curtains open wide. Beatrice needs a lot of light on things.

Beatrice climbs the trailer steps *stomp stomp stomp* and the whole trailer shakes. She bangs the door open-shut and drops into her seat.

"Sorry I'm late."

Today Beatrice is wearing tall jeans that come up over her shoulders. They have the letters "HEE-HAW" on them. Cartoons of chickens and donkeys in straw hats are there too. These jeans smell musty, like a warehouse. She's also got on a blue-sky tank top and boots with teeth on the bottom.

Humans choose such interesting bandannas to wear. My bandanna is practical: it lets others know that I'm a therapy dog, and it allows everyone full petting access to my soft silver fur. Humans' bandannas don't seem to serve any real purpose. They must be hot and they definitely constrict jumping. I mean, when's the last time you saw a human jump just for the joy of jumping?

Tessa bursts with laughter. "Bea! Where in the world did you get those overalls?"

Beatrice's face breaks into a wide grin, and the air shimmers with glee. She slides her fingers under the straps on her shoulders. "You like these? Got them off eBay. Only cost twelve bucks. They say 'Hee-Haw.'"

"I see that. My grandmother used to love that show."

"It was a show?"

Tessa chuckles. "It was. Look it up on YouTube."

"Can't. Grounded from YouTube."

"Ahhh. Want to talk about it?"

"No." Beatrice knocks her knuckles on the table next to her. She leaps up, squats down. Beatrice is an uncomfortable tight knot today. The trailer sways with her every move. "Hi, Luna."

I wag. Loosen her a bit.

She scratches me under my chin—*ahhhhh*. I lean into the scratch, farther, farther, until I lose my balance and topple over. Beatrice wrinkles her nose with delight and rubs my belly. Tessa pulls a ball off a shelf. No, not a ball; a balloon. One with a rubber band attached. She hands it to Beatrice. She must sense that Bea is tighter than usual today too. "Punch the balloon. Go on. Give it a whack or two while we chat."

Beatrice narrows her eyes a bit, but she clutches the rubber band in her fist and immediately punches; *whang whang whang* shouts the balloon. It bounces back and forth off her fist like a maniacal game of fetch. I don't love the movement, the sound, the smell of this rubber balloon bouncing around our small trailer. But it seems to be loosening Bea's knot. Tessa knows her clients well.

Tessa clears her throat, takes a deep breath. "What did you think about the group session? I thought it went—"

"I like it when it's just me and you, Ms. Tessa," Beatrice says. *Whang whang whang* moans the balloon.

Tessa smiles. "I like that too. But, Beatrice, you've made a lot of progress lately."

"Have I?" When Beatrice asks this question, the air singes around the edges, a slow burn. Smoky. *Whang whang whang.*

Tessa's eyes soften. I mirror her. Beatrice stops pounding that infernal balloon and drapes an arm over my neck. She's heavier today than most days.

"You have, Bea," Tessa says. "So listen. I want to

24

continue these group counseling sessions. And I think you're a perfect fit."

"No."

Tessa chuckles but shifts in her seat. "I didn't ask all my clients, Bea. Just a few who I thought would really benefit from being around others."

The air feels thick with smoke now, and doubt hangs over Beatrice like a heavy blanket. I nudge her with my nose, my skull. I lick her. I waggle closer to her, let my tongue loll out. Beatrice smiles. Loosens further.

"Luna will still be there, right?"

Absolutely.

"Absolutely."

Beatrice grinds her teeth. A knot tightening. "Do you think that kid's hoverboard really floats, Ms. Tessa?"

Tessa beams. "I believe what Hector tells us, yes. I'm excited to see it."

I don't fully understand. But it sounds like it's really important to Beatrice to see something float, so it is important to me too.

"So you'll be there?" Tessa asks. She's smart to ask this, because Beatrice has not yet said yes, and Beatrice can be sneaky about these things.

Beatrice lies down on the floor of the trailer next to

me. Squeezes me tight. Whispers into my fur, "I kinda hated that last one."

But Tessa's tiny human ears didn't hear. "What?"

Beatrice leaps off the floor, back into her chair. Knocks her knuckles on the side table. *Knock knock knot.* "Remind that kid to bring his hoverboard, Ms. Tessa."

★ 4 ★

AMELIA THE SHADOW

The wind rustles, and Amelia slips inside the trailer. Tessa finishes pouring herself a cup of mud and turns. Leaps like a kitten. "Oh! Amelia! I didn't hear you come in!"

Amelia glides across the trailer to me, drops to her knees, and droops over me. Some days Amelia has tears. Some days she just needs to breathe in my fur. Today is a fur-breathing day. Her hair is twined like a tug-of-war rope around and over the top of her head and I love her and we breathe each other's fur.

Amelia is a shadow. Shadows are either in front of you or behind you. Amelia is a behind-you shadow. I think she'd smile more if she could be an in-front-of-you

27

shadow. She could use the reminder of her shadow stretching long before her.

Tessa crosses to her granny's lace curtains and closes them. Sunlight pokes through the old holes, polka-dotting the room. Shadows appreciate this play of light.

"How did speech therapy go yesterday, Amelia?" Tessa asks, as gently as dandelion fluff. "Did you work on saying *Luna* like we discussed?"

Amelia shrugs. She closes her eyes. Purple circles bloom underneath them. They burn with tired; I can feel my own eyes echo hers. Amelia does not sleep well. The nightmares won't let her. She squeezes me tighter.

Shadows are the most loyal friend you can have.

"So, the group counseling earlier this week," Tessa says. "What did you think?" The way Tessa asks this—a song in her words, her body balanced on the edge of her seat—it's easy to see she wants a *yes I enjoyed it* nod from Amelia.

The hug Amelia's giving me tightens. The air in the trailer tightens. The lines on Amelia's face tighten. But she doesn't respond. I nuzzle her under her chin, trying to prompt her to nod *yes*. She leans back and looks at me with a twinkle in her eye, like she knows what I'm doing, like she caught me sneaking extra treats.

"I think that kind of interaction with others your

age could bring you to the next level of progress, Amelia," Tessa says, sipping her mud. Amelia and I both hear the words that Tessa isn't saying, floating fat and lazy like bubbles: *Maybe they can get you to talk again?*

"I'd like for you to join us for the next one." Tessa offers Amelia an Oreo, her favorite. "What do you say?"

Amelia knows if she takes the cookie, she's agreeing to come again. This is how she talks now—agreeing and disagreeing only. It must be so hard to do that. There are so many things that don't require either. That require both.

Amelia slides her gaze my way, and I nudge her arm: *Go on. Take it.* Amelia narrows her eyes at me—she feels *doubtful*—but sighs, takes the cookie.

Tessa beams. "Great! I'm excited for you and the others to get to know one another better."

Amelia grins, and she has Oreo goop stuck to her front teeth, making her look positively defenseless. But Tessa snickers. She stands to go get another cup of mud.

Amelia flings her arms around my neck again. This time, though, the hug is salty. Damp. Heavy. She agreed but she wanted to disagree. She's doing this for Tessa. For me. And I understand this; it is duty.

Sometimes Amelia feels—and so I feel—*worry*. Sick-to-your-stomach, thoughts-spinning-like-a-tornado worry. Eating-too-much-green-grass-and-horking-it-up worry. *Worry* is questions with no answers. Today Amelia's question feels like *will this group make me forget?*

I stand tall, my fur absorbing Amelia's tears. It's like watching someone's heart thump, letting them cry while wrapped in their hug. I don't know if Tessa sees Amelia's tears, feels her worry.

Humans have awful eyes. A lot of times humans don't see what's in the shadows.

★ 5 ★

CALEB THE WATERFALL

Rushing water is odd, because it both roars and makes the sound *shhhhh*. Quiet and loud. Relaxing and powerful. Water gives us everything, and it can take everything away if it wants too.

Caleb is just as full of opposites. He enters the trailer smiling, gives a curt nod to Tessa. "Good morning, Ms. Tessa." Then to me, "And to you, Luna." He perches on the edge of his chair and bounces his knees.

Caleb doesn't pet me, not really. Sometimes he'll pat my head. And sometimes, when the air around him stops rushing and spinning, he will take a corner of my ear and rub it between his thumb and forefinger. I try not to take it personally. Caleb interacts with his environment as little as possible. That is the opposite of rushing water. But he's definitely a waterfall. He plows forward at a pace that's both blurry and forceful.

Tessa pauses at her lace curtains. Open or closed for Caleb? She settles on halfway. Caleb is good at compromise.

Caleb and Tessa play chess. Sometimes they mention horses, and I grumble because I've been told that horses can be dangerous. But these are just tiny plastic things, so I don't understand what damage they can do. When I grumble it makes Caleb smile. It's not easy to make Caleb smile. He's too busy moving.

While they play, they talk about things called parents and divorce. His parents shout a lot now, he says. Shouting is like getting kicked with words, so I understand why he's sad about it. Tessa suggests some things and Caleb says "I guess so" and "I'll try" a lot. I guess these are his duty.

"Checkmate," Caleb says, leaning back at last. He stretches sideways to another small table and, *squirt squirt*, he coats his hands in this clear goo that smells like steely sharp needles. He rubs his hands vigorously, and I wince along with him because his hands are red raw and this stuff *stings*. Now Caleb allows himself a treat: he dips his hand into one of Tessa's glass jars and gets a single wrapped candy. Caleb is always the one who says checkmate, but they still play every time. It seems silly to me to do this, but humans do so many silly things.

Tessa nods, Caleb chews, I lie down. Caleb is tall like a man-human but his face is still soft like a boy-human. He feels weird about this. We sometimes feel like we don't fit inside our own body.

"I've been reading more about therapy dogs, Ms. Tessa," Caleb says at last. He doesn't look at me but he's talking about me? "There are a lot of opinions out there if they're truly effective."

Effective. I don't know this word but something in the way Caleb says it stings like goo on red, raw hands.

Tessa smiles. "I'm glad you've been looking into it. I'm not all that worried about Luna being *effective*. If she makes you happy, she's doing her job."

Caleb blinks. He doesn't seem to understand this duty of mine.

"So what did you think of our first group counseling session?" Tessa asks. "I'd like for you to return. Maybe someone there can finally beat you at chess."

Tessa titters, Caleb does not. He blinks. The air rushes like wind over water.

"I'm not sure that's the best direction to take, Ms. Tessa," he says. "I'm very comfortable with where we are now."

Tessa smiles warmly, and the air around Caleb calms. She can do that; she can smile like a sunflower turning to the sky and the wind somehow settles. "Oh, I am too. But comfortable isn't really where we grow."

And then Caleb does something he's never done before. He looks at me and says, "Will Luna be there again too?"

I thought Caleb never cared if I was there or not. I thought he'd never really noticed me beyond a small pat or tiny tug or an offering of a bowl of water. I thought he believed I wasn't *effective*. Sometimes, something shifts—a tree falls, a mudslide occurs—and a rushing river is forced to take a different route through the dark woods. Caleb's river just took a new route.

"Definitely," Tessa says. "Luna is always by our side."

I am. I am always by your side, I promise. This part of duty comes easy to me.

Caleb doesn't pet me, doesn't tug my ears. He stands, nods at Tessa. He douses his red, raw hands with a squirt of that clear goo. He rubs the goo all over his palms. Together we wince.

"I'll try again. Just once though. One more try."

★ 6 ★

HECTOR THE RIVER ROCK

A river rock anchors itself in earth, and what might have been sharp edges are now honed. Chipped off by the world. Worn down, you might even say. But stubborn. Steadfast. River rocks wish only to plant themselves in a go go go world.

Hector is just such a rock. He's used to everyone else's pace feeling different from his. So after he enters the trailer with his bike in tow (he always wrestles his bike into this tiny space), Tessa asks, "Group counseling again?" Hector just shrugs and says, "All right."

For Hector, the lace curtains are closed tight. Sunlight still seeps through the holes, but it's mostly dark. Hector likes calm dark.

"Can you bring your hoverboard?" Tessa asks. "I know it's likely bulky, but Beatrice is really excited to see it."

"I'll bring the hoverboard," he says. "That girl needs to see it float."

He lays his dark furry head on my belly and closes his eyes. We're tired, I feel. Not sleepy. *Weary.* My eyes droop and burn. I yawn. And we agree to whatever Tessa asks, because that's easiest.

★ 7 ★

NOTHING IN COMMON EXCEPT

Humans move through time by slicing it into seconds, minutes, hours. Dogs move through time in a rainbow of colors: days begin with pink, then yellow, then white, orange, lilac, blue, purple, black. Humans would see a lot more beauty in their world if they saw it through rainbows instead of timepieces.

Tessa and I move through several rainbows before another group meeting with the Knot, the Shadow, the Waterfall, the Rock. This time Tessa places a chessboard, a deck of cards, and some clackety dice on the tables. "We'll play some games first, then we'll move into doing a group sand tray," she tells me. She tells herself.

Caleb arrives first and sets up the chessboard,

gingerly placing the pieces on their squares in a way that reminds me of when Tessa says, "Stay, Luna." He sits, lean and knobby as a pile of sticks, waiting for an opponent. I sit next to him, as erect as he sits. We feel as jittery as crickets.

"Has Luna had dinner, Ms. Tessa?" Caleb asks. He looks at her, not me.

Tessa smiles. "She has! Thank you for asking about her, Caleb."

He nods once, like he can check that item off a list he has inside his head.

Amelia and Beatrice squeeze through the doorway at the same time. "Dude. Sorry about that green paint," Beatrice says to Amelia. "I really did like your painting." Beatrice has new hair today, a pop of pink like Tessa's bubble gum.

Amelia shrugs but smiles down at her cowboy boots. Her sundress swirls around her as she sits near the cards and begins sorting them by their pictures. She twines her fingers into the ropes that wind around her head.

Tessa looks at her wrist-collar, the one that slices up the seconds. "I guess we should go ahead and get started—"

"Whoa, whoa, whoa," Beatrice says, knocking her knuckles on the table. "Where's the other dude? The kid with the bike?"

"Hector," Tessa says. "I'm not sure. But it's time for us to start, and—"

"I bet that hoverboard of his doesn't work," Beatrice says, leaning back in her chair. "So he's blowing us off. Just didn't come! Hmmph. I didn't know that was an option."

Caleb nibbles his lip. He is trying not to say the words that sit on his tongue, but rushing water often can't be stopped. "No one's forcing you to be here."

Beatrice snorts. Leans farther back in her chair and balances one shoe on the opposite knee. She is showing the others the teeth on her shoes, and it makes me think of growling dogs.

"Au contraire, friend," Beatrice says. "My mom is most definitely forcing me to be here."

A little prick stabs Tessa at that remark, a jab from a thorn. "We're all here to learn and grow. Now, before we begin, I have to tell you—"

Shouting from upstairs slices through the air like a sharp knife. "What are you doing here, Steve? This isn't your night! I have Caleb on Tuesdays!"

Caleb sits even more erect, if that's possible. I know from past meetings that this is Caleb's mother's voice. He burns like a hot road. I move toward him, unsure if he wants me near.

Footsteps pound overhead. Another voice, a man.

39

"You thought you could just change him over to group counseling and not tell me?" This is Caleb's father speaking. Shouting.

"Steve, his counselor recommended . . ." The next few shouts are muffled by footsteps and moving furniture. A chair? I cock my head at Caleb. His neck is taut, but he shows no emotion. The rush of water inside him is strong, drowning out everything else.

All eyes in this basement look up to the grungy water-stained ceiling. All eyes avoid looking at each other.

Tessa crumples like a ball of paper, hearing the yelling from above. She clears her throat. "So, kids," she begins. "This obviously isn't ideal, but—"

"Surely one-on-one counseling would be better . . . ," Caleb's father yells, then fades. There is more pounding of feet, more grumbling of voice.

"Hey, listen, I agree," says a different woman's voice through the ceiling. "If my insurance would keep covering the one-on-one sessions, you bet your sweet bippy my girl would be in those. There's not even enough chairs in this crappy room for all of us to sit and wait."

Beatrice pushes up suddenly from the table, her metal chair screeching like a hawk as she shoves it backward. She jabs a finger at the ceiling. "My mother, ladies and gentlemen." This knot is tight.

Now a fourth voice chimes in from upstairs, another male voice: "Everyone, everyone! No need to shout. Quiet down. Quiet down."

At this Amelia stands, gestures at the voice through the ceiling, and curtsies with her long, flowy skirt. Bowing, I think humans call it, but this doesn't seem playful like a dog's bow. Caleb sucks in a sharp breath. Amelia and Beatrice doing this, each claiming their own yelling voice, has somehow slowed the rush of water in his head. But no one dares talk. The Knot, the Shadow, the Waterfall: all await the next shout from above. There always seems to be another shout from above.

Tessa senses how much these yelling adults are dampening her session, staining it like the rusty water blots staining the ceiling overhead. As the voices continue shouting, she stands. She's an angry bee, buzzing mad, which is rare for Tessa. "I'm going to tell them to quiet down, okay? Their behavior is an unwelcome interruption. Please, go ahead and start playing a few games. I will be two minutes."

Tessa dashes up the stairs two at a time, saying, "Excuse me, folks? We need to chat a second. . . ."

Beatrice cracks her knuckles, surveys the room. I try to get a read on her, but she's clenched tighter than a fist. She stalks to a bright red plastic hook on the wall, pushes her sleeves up to her elbows. "If I pull the fire alarm, that'll hush 'em up."

The Shadow shrinks, folds in on herself. Amelia does something I've never heard her do: she wails like an injured puppy. Shakes her head. No; shakes her whole body. Her eyes are wide, her face pale and clammy. I dash to her side, lean against her. We are all pulse and saliva.

Beatrice holds her hands up, palms out. "I'm sorry, I'm sorry!" she says, walking backward away from the red plastic. "I won't do that. I promise. I'll . . ." She scans the room again, a hawk searching prey. She spots it.

Beatrice pushes one of the white plastic tables, and it moans across the concrete floor. It slams against the far wall. Amelia has collapsed into a nearby chair, but she's stumbled away from the blister of panic and is now watching the Knot pull tight.

Caleb picks at the hem of his cargo shorts. "What are you doing?"

Beatrice grabs one of the screaming metal chairs and places it on top of the table. She tests her shaky creation, then climbs up this pyramid. It wobbles and sways. She clicks the latch on the small dirty window near the basement ceiling and props it open. Hot Texas air pushes inside. It matches Beatrice's anger.

"I'm going to find that kid. That . . . Herman."

"Hector," Caleb says. His forehead crinkles. "Why? To see a crummy hoverboard?"

"YES, to see a crummy hoverboard!" Beatrice snaps.

She is standing on a chair on a table on the floor, and she wobbles. This whole decision wobbles. Alarm blooms in Beatrice's chest as she sways atop the chair, but she regains her balance. Beatrice always somehow regains her balance. I love her for that.

"No," she says, changing her mind from the top of her creation. Humans do that a lot: say yes and no to the same thing. "Because I'm sick and tired of people claiming to be something they're not! Because I'm sick and tired of people giving up on me!" She realizes that was too loud, though, because she pauses for a moment, breathes, and her voice drops to a low, hissing whisper. "That kid was so excited to show us his invention. Don't you want to know why he blew us off? Don't you want to know why he doesn't want to be friends with us?"

The three of them stand in silence, a tense triangle: the Knot teetering high above them, the Shadow and the Waterfall looking up at her. Those three things— Knot, Shadow, Waterfall—have very little in common.

Except, perhaps, this. This wondering: *Why does everyone give up on me?* Because the Shadow now nods. Amelia's jaw is taut, and she nods. *Yes.* Yes, she too wants to know why Hector doesn't want to be friends.

Beatrice beams, scrambles through the basement window. Her tank top rips on the rusty metal frame as she scrambles out, and she mutters a word that makes Caleb blink repeatedly.

Amelia scales the table-chair mountain as though she were made of air, and she hoists herself gently out the window.

This is far, far outside of the routine Tessa and I have built. My tail droops with worry.

The Knot and the Shadow lean back through the window. "You in?" the Knot says to the Waterfall. "Because if you are, you gotta come *now*. I figure we've got about two more minutes before Tessa finds out we're gone. She and our parents will come looking for us."

Caleb chews on his bottom lip. Looks at me. Looks at the window. "My parents won't come looking for me," Caleb mutters, and he begins to climb. He really doesn't need the chair; he's tall enough to pull himself through the window just by standing on the table. "Do you even know where Hector lives?" he asks as he kicks his legs to propel himself up.

No no no! I plead. My clients—my *humans*—have found the broken place in the fence where they can escape. They are puppies, scampering away, far from home, and *they're not even chipped*! How will they find their way?

I have to go with them. I can't let them wander away without me. It is my duty to protect them. I made a promise to do exactly that when I began my training. Plus, my heart is too twined with their hearts. I whine and leap atop the table. It wobbles, sways, and I whimper more. The plastic feels cold and weird on my paw pads.

"Luna, NO!" Beatrice says, looking inside at me teetering on the table. "Stay!" She gently lowers the window back down. Through the glass I can see their feet still standing there, I can feel them figuring out their plan.

"You're not our dog, Luna! Stay!" Caleb says. That part stings. Of course I'm their dog.

I'm their dog.

If I go with them, I will most certainly give up all the credits that I've earned toward being a therapy dog. I am four visits away, three if this meeting counts. A whisker away. *Almost*.

Will they still let me be a therapy dog if I go?

Will they let me be one if I *don't*?

I try to remember if we covered runaway clients in my training. My instinct tells me: I can't let them just wander away. These clients, these humans—I love them. They are my pack. My duty. They are still full of holes that haven't yet been filled, and my job is to fill them. To guide them. My job is to be their moon.

I jump atop the chair, and it trembles like a mad dog. I have a choice: leap for the window or crash to the floor.

I *leap*. My front paws and head push through the still-unlatched window. The edge of it crashes against my shoulders. My back legs kick kick kick frantically, and I knock over the chair. It clatter-crashes to the basement floor.

"Luna!" Caleb and Beatrice both shout. They realize they have to pull me through to join them, rather than let me fall backward onto the hard concrete floor. They tug and pull. I kick and whine. And I make it through.

But there's no time to catch my breath. Beatrice looks in at the mess I made kicking over the chair. "Tessa's coming," she whispers as we hear footsteps inside. "Let's *go*!"

And we run.

* 8 *

PICKLE PRESSURE

We run downhill, down a wide, paved road covered in Texas grit. Cars parked in a large lot bounce sunlight all around, looking like a cluster of stars and amplifying the heat. Candy-colored storefronts blare music and people bang out drumbeats on plastic buckets. I feel Amelia's heart pull toward the rhythm. Food smells tickle the air: tacos and pastries and burgers.

"Luna," Beatrice huffs. "You can't come with us. Go *away*."

I can't leave them. I know my duty.

Humans sleep in doorways and slump against street signs. I try to feel what they feel, these tired humans asleep on the streets, but the emotion around them is fuzzy static, as hard to sort through as sand. My forehead wrinkles; I hope they find the rest they need.

When I glance back up the street, past our yellow church on the hill, I see Austin's famous pink dome peeking between sleek skyscrapers. Tessa always smiles at that dome when it catches her eye. She calls it the Texas State Capitol, says with breathy awe that it's the largest state capitol building in the U.S.

"Luna!"

I hear Tessa's voice weave around buildings, slice through smells. *My* heart pulls to *it*. But the kids must hear it too, because Amelia grabs Beatrice's wrist and pulls her into a tight, stale alley. It is wet with things other than this morning's rainwater, dotted with fuzzy mushrooming cigarette butts. Caleb shudders to run through this grime, but he follows. Amelia splashes through this alley and pushes against each of the doors. At last, one is open, and she scoots through a creaky wooden entrance, still gripping Beatrice by the wrist. Caleb and I follow.

Inside, in the dark, we pant, both me and my humans. Caleb looks at his mud-spattered shoes and mutters, "Aw man! I left my backpack back there."

This darkness is odd. My spine tingles. My fur prickles. A grumble rolls around in my belly.

The kids press their backs against the wall, suck in

48

heaving breaths. I can sense the goose bumps that rise on their skin as their weak human eyes adjust to this dark, dark room.

"What IS this place?" Caleb breathes.

The light in here is blue-black, and it makes all the colors look juicy. Overripe. The pinks burn too pink, the greens glow. The lights point up at a looming massive beast, peering through tall grass with wide eyes and huge nostrils and giant, grabbing hands.

Amelia stumbles backward. This monster? So . . . musty. I sneeze: *wachooo!*

Beatrice reaches up, slowly, slowly, toward the beast. I growl. She looks at me, winks. "It's okay, Luna."

Beatrice knocks *thump thump* on the beast's plastic nose. "King Kong," she says. "How'd you get in here?"

"Better question," says Caleb's muffled voice from around a curtained corner. "How do we get out?"

It is a dark maze, this building, and around every corner is another odd beast: A human with sharp, pointy teeth. "'Sup, Dracula?" Beatrice says, flicking her thumb against one of his fangs. A thing that is half-man, half-dog. "Wolfman! Always a treat. Milk-Bone dog biscuit treats, to be exact." A beast in an odd helmet, with too-long arms. "High five, aqua dude. Or, well, high three," she says, reaching down to smack his weird, webbed fingers.

At every turn, my hackles rise, and another figure looms. But they're all still. Plastic. Dusty. Fake. We pass a display with a small wooden box inside and a sign that Caleb reads aloud: "'Museum of the Weird employees: never, ever, ever open this box!'" He cocks his head like a puppy. "Museum of the Weird. People pay to see this stuff?"

"Dude, I would so open that box if I worked here," Beatrice says. Amelia giggles.

More turns, and the light fades from blue-black to yellowy-orange. We pass a set of bookshelves that, my ears tell me, is hollow on the other side; it opens into another room. A small human head with odd, stretched skin and frizzy hair perches behind glass. Fingers and teeth and oddly shaped animals are all on display. It is frightening and confusing and I growl at each turn, but my humans don't seem to be scared. They cringe and stare at these objects, but they seem to be as fascinated as a dog with a bone.

Beatrice stops short in front of a display of a piglet with one eye and no snout. It has an odd trunk-like thing sprouting from its forehead. She is *apprehensive*; her scent is like oniony grass. And yet she stays planted, staring.

Amelia peers around the corner ahead and, seeing

no one, whips her blue screen out of the bag resting on her hip. She taps on the screen several times, then shows it to Caleb.

"Hector has an Instagram account?" he says. "He looks younger than thirteen. But good thinking."

They flick the screen with their fingertips, Caleb leaning tall over Amelia's shoulder; he has to hunch to see. The screen turns their faces blue.

Meanwhile Beatrice tightens and tightens, staring at this pig. Her throat closes. Her teeth clench. Her fingernails dig into her palms. I nudge her. *Hey, you okay?* She scratches the top of my head but never looks away from this odd tiny pig with its one eye, its small, elephant-like trunk.

Sometimes at home, Tessa tries to open a jar of pickles, and the lid is on so tight, it takes all of her might to open it. And when she does, the jar shouts *pop*! That same pressure builds inside Beatrice, I feel.

Amelia gasps suddenly, a tiny peep of inspiration like a balloon squeak, and points at several things on the screen. Caleb nods.

"I see what you're saying," he says, which is funny because Amelia says nothing. "That tower. That's the moonlight tower in Zilker Park. Looks like Hector flies a drone there a lot."

Amelia beams, nods. My soul sings alongside hers. It's been a long time since someone has understood her like that.

They scroll and point, point and scroll. They nod their blue faces. Beatrice stares at a pig and builds toward a *pop*. That scares me, so I lick her knuckles. She doesn't seem to notice.

"Look at that one," Caleb says, pointing to the screen. "He posted it yesterday. I can't read Spanish though. This word here, *mañana*. That means tomorrow. So . . . today." Caleb tosses over his shoulder: "Hey. Beatrice. Can you read Spanish?"

She shakes her head. "French . . ." she says in a murmur, eyes never leaving the display.

Amelia's lips purse. She is suddenly stubborn, like a mosquito buzzing near your ear. I can smell her frustration: Why didn't Caleb ask *her* if *she* can read Spanish? She pokes at the screen.

"Oh, the hashtag!" Caleb says as the screen flickers. "Good idea. Let's see what this Bad to the Drone Piloting Club is all about."

They scroll a bit more, and Caleb gasps. Points. Amelia grins.

"They're doing a thing! Tonight! Hector will be at Zilker Park tonight! Starting at seven, until nine, it looks like? They're doing a nighttime photography meetup." His eyes rise to Amelia's. "Do you know how to get there? I have a general idea, but . . ."

Amelia pokes the screen a few more times, and I gag, thinking how dirty that screen must be. Human fingers are the grossest. She turns the screen toward Caleb.

"Google Maps. Nice. Okay, so according to this"— Caleb squints at the screen—"Zilker is about three miles away. Not bad. We should be there in less than an hour?"

Caleb looks at the collar strapped around his wrist. "It's almost seven now. If we hustle, we'll get there right in the middle of the meetup."

Amelia slides her phone back into the bag on her hip and jerks her head toward the whiter light at the front of the building. She wisps around a corner. The Shadow is gone.

Caleb nods once, reaches out to wake Beatrice. As his fingers inch closer, closer to her, I realize: this is the *pop*. I try to step in between them, but—

"Hey, we know where we're headed," Caleb says. And just as his fingers graze her arm, she—*pop!*— slams her fist back and up, directly into Caleb's nose. A sickening crack fills this tiny space.

Blood spatters everywhere, all at once, like a firework. "What the *heck*?" Caleb covers his nose, but blood seeps through his fingers. "What'd you do that for!"

Beatrice jams her fists against her cheeks and swipes furiously. Tears? I'm so confused by all these emotions swelling into this small space, filling it like thick smoke, choking us. None of this is what I've trained for. I spin and twist, trying to decide who to comfort first.

Beatrice mutters a word that makes Caleb blink even more than the punch. "Dude. Reflex. I—I—*here*." Beatrice grabs a corner of the musty velvet curtain lining this space behind the displays. "Sit. Tilt your head back."

Caleb sinks to the sticky wooden floor and Beatrice mops his face with the curtain. He can't help it: his face contorts. She pinches his nose, tilts his chin to the ceiling. Words are clogged in her throat: *I'm sorry.* They're making her as sick as a cat with a hair ball. But she doesn't cough them up.

Through his pinched nose and the velvet curtain, Caleb's voice sounds squeaky and muffled. "Were you crying?"

The Knot pulls tight. "Do you want me to—"

But here's the thing: the Knot breathes, loosens,

and stops herself from saying the rest of that sentence, *punch you again?*

Tessa was smart to start this group. It's already changing them.

Tessa! My heart twinges, thinking of her, shouting my name. But I know I'm supposed to be here, with these three. I know they need me by their side. This is my duty, I'm sure of it.

"Ugh, where is this curtain from?" Caleb says through a swollen nose. "It smells like a coffin."

Beatrice laughs one short burst. "You know what a coffin smells like?"

Caleb holds up a corner of the blood-soaked, dusty velvet. "This. I'm certain it smells like this."

Beatrice beams at him. We—she and I—feel *grateful* that Caleb isn't the kind of person who holds too much of a grudge after getting socked in the nose.

"Zilker Park," Caleb says, his voice muffled. "Hector will be at Zilker Park tonight. Until nine."

Beatrice leaps to her feet, her boots loud on this floor. She re-knots the flannel shirt tied around her waist, offers Caleb a hand up. He eyes it. But he takes it.

They glance back at the bloodstained curtain, the drops of blood on the floor.

"They should charge folks extra to see that," Caleb

says. Beatrice throws her head back and guffaws. Laughter through tears. In a matter of minutes, Caleb has loosened the Knot.

I am tail-chasing confused by all this. But you know what also happens when you chase your tail? Besides confusion, I mean? Joy. Joy, sweet and juicy as lemonade.

★9★

HOPE IS A STAR

We wind our way to the front of the Museum of the Weird, passing a woman with bright pink lips perched behind a desk like a parrot. We freeze. She shouts, "Where'd you kids come from? Hey! Did you pay?"

Amelia, Beatrice, Caleb, and I push and trip and fall over each other to get away from this angry-eyebrows woman. She grabs a bat from under the desk and dashes around it, chasing us. "Hey!"

We leap and tumble through the front door. Another plastic human is perched at the storefront: a pirate made of bones, sitting on a treasure chest, swigging from a bottle. Beatrice nicks him on the chin as we dash past:

"Quite the crew you got in there, matey!"

We runrunrun down the street, the woman waving the bat over her head and yelling, "Cheapskate kids!" She doesn't chase us far, though. We duck into a shady alley to catch our breath, and Beatrice looks down at me.

"Should we take Luna with us?" she asks. "Is that like stealing, if she comes with us all the way to Zilker Park?"

Caleb's forehead wrinkles. "Maybe." He stoops to my eye level, points back up the hill, to the steeple poking above the rest of the buildings. "Luna, head back, okay? You're not our dog."

I don't know why they keep saying that. Of course I'm their dog. And I'm not leaving them. I know my duty.

We stumble out of the alley. Amelia stops short, gasps. I follow her eyes up, into the pale orange sky now tinged with soft purple. Glimmering ahead, down the hill, over the lake, is a massive shimmering rainbow. It is almost a full arch, stretching from the shiny silver skyscrapers to the lush green park on the opposite side of the water.

Caleb twitches. Scratches his head. The neck of his crisp T-shirt underneath his crisp button shirt is stained with blood. He tugs at it absentmindedly. He doesn't like wearing this stained shirt. "It is nice, isn't it?"

Beatrice slides her eyes at Amelia, and they share a secret smile. "Yes, indeedy, Mr. Rogers. It sure is keen." Beatrice's voice has a tease tied to it, like a bacon treat stuffed deep inside a Kong toy.

But Caleb doesn't notice. He twitches again. Stretches the neck of his shirt farther. "It's just a trick of light. Isn't that wild? It's not even *there*, but we can see it. How can something both exist and not exist?"

Beatrice blinks. It takes a lot to make Beatrice blink. This is like a tennis ball *ping!* on this moment. "I know how," she says. The tease in her voice is gone.

That rainbow, it somehow reminds me of the many colors of feelings Beatrice just went through inside: from blue through purple, to pink, into yellow. A rainbow is just like that. A rainbow is laughter through tears. It's all the colors of a day, crammed into a few moments.

The Shadow, the Knot, and the Waterfall take a minute to figure out which way we're headed. They look at Amelia's screen, then up at the street signs.

"Left," Beatrice says.

"No, that's east," Caleb says. He gently turns Amelia's wrist to point her phone down the street. "We need to head west. Southwest, actually. I think."

"You don't know?"

"Well, no, I'm not *certain*. But I think." Caleb bites his lip. He looks at the map on the screen again.

"So we're headed in a direction you *think* is right?"

"You got a better idea?"

Beatrice cracks her knuckles. "Well, yeah. We take off in the direction I say. And FAST."

"Going fast in the wrong direction won't help," Caleb says, head cocked. "Hector will only be at Zilker until nine. We don't have a lot of time here, Beatrice. . . ."

While they bicker, I take the opportunity to open up my nostrils and taste the air. Rain is hanging nearby. Cigarettes. More food and humans. And . . .

Cat.

He slinks up to the four of us. One-eyed, he is, like the pirate made of bones behind us. The cat would be orange, I think, if he weren't so dirty. He is sticky and thin, but not sickly. He does all right for a cat.

Greetings, dog, he purrs. *Might you have tuna?*

Tuna? Cats are so annoying. *No, of course I don't have tuna.*

My trio of clients begins walking down a street they call Sixth, checking the map Amelia has on her blue screen. I follow. The cat, unfortunately, does the same.

The street is gritty, dusty, and lined with small

trees. Dozens of pigeons strut bravely up to us, warbling, *French fry? Got a french fry? French fry?* When we don't offer them food, they scowl and poop and flutter to the next group of humans: *French fry? Got a french fry?*

The cat hisses at them. The birds cuss and strut away. The cat weaves in front of me. *So what's the story here, huh?* he purrs. *You and these kids. Are you part of a revenge story? A fable? A mystery?* The cat swishes his ratty tail at my humans. *A group of kids and their dog, solving crimes. So cliché.*

I do not answer because I do not like the way this cat rolls his one eye at the word *cliché*. Also I do not know the word *cliché*.

Where are you headed? The cat's voice sounds like sandpaper.

Southwest, I say, pretending I know exactly what that means. In my experience, you can't let a cat see your weaknesses. *Zilker Park.*

Ah, a true destination! the cat says. He looks over his shoulder, like he's leaving something behind. *It appears we have a quest!*

A quest? The question slips from me before I can stop myself. Drat!

Indeed, a quest! The cat scans my humans with his

one eye. *By the look of things we are currently near the beginning of Act Two, correct? Solidly in the Belly of the Whale, as old Campbell would say. Ha! An excellent time to introduce a new character. Pssst. That's me, dog.*

My forehead crinkles. *Act Two?*

The cat ignores my confusion. *And have we had our Call to Adventure? Did you heed it? Or did you leap into this voyage without much forethought?*

This cat speaks pure gibberish. He makes me feel *agitated*, itchy and jumpy like I'm loaded down with fleas.

The cat sighs at my silence. *What are we seeking on our quest, Protagonist?*

I don't know what that word means, *protagonist*. I reckon it has something to do with dog tags. So I stall. *What do you mean, seeking?*

The cat rolls his one eye again. We are trotting down Sixth at a nice clip, and I don't really have time for this conversation.

Seeking! the sandpaper cat says. He darts in and out behind things: garbage cans and small trees and newspaper stands. He is good at remaining hidden. *What is our goal on this quest?* When I don't answer right away, Sandpaper sighs heavily and says, *Why are we going to Zilker Park?*

We? I huff.

Well, yes, Sandpaper says, darting behind a bike rack, then out again. *Your quest needs a narrator, obviously.*

A narrator, I say. Again, I'm as lost as a dog with no scent trail, but I can't admit this to a cat.

Yes, a narrator! The one who tells the story long after you're dead and gone?

Dead? I croak. *Gone?* How long does this cat think this . . . quest . . . is going to take? I choke: *KAK!*

Amelia turns back at my cough. Sandpaper darts behind the leg of a bench, unseen. Amelia smiles, I smile, we keep walking.

Sandpaper catches up to me. *You're not really familiar with how quests work, are you?*

I guess not.

So what is it we seek, Protagonist?

My name is Luna. And . . . um . . . a boy. A Hector Vasquez.

Sandpaper pauses for a half beat. *Hector Vasquez. I see. Is he missing?*

Missing? I repeat. *I guess to Beatrice, yes. He is.*

We walk for another moment in silence before I hear it again, floating on the edge of the wind: "LUNA?"

Tessa!

My heart yanks me backward toward her voice like a pop of a leash.

Sandpaper must've heard it too, because he grins wide, whiskers showcasing his catty mirth. *Ah yes. Entering our story just in time. Followers of our fair quest, may I introduce: our antagonists.*

Ants? What are you talking about? I ask.

Sandpaper flicks a fluff of spiderweb from his whisker. *Here we are, on the lam—*

Now you're talking about sheep? I interrupt.

Protagonist, the cat says, *our Merry Band of Five is being pursued by the bad guys.*

FOUR, I snap at this cat. *It's a Merry Band of FOUR, thank you. And those aren't bad guys.*

No? Sandpaper asks. *Then why are we running?*

This cat asks hard questions. Tessa is *not* a bad guy. But I look at my clients and they're most definitely running. *I don't know,* I say at last.

The cat slithers between the ankles of people who don't even notice he's there. *Well, one thing's for certain. This group needs a hero. Lucky I came along.*

Me! I bark, then I lower my voice to a growl. *The hero is going to be me, cat.* I can't explain to this cat about duty right now.

The cat blinks. Or maybe, because he has only one

64

eye, he winks? *Good news, dog. The protagonist usually IS the hero of the tale.*

I nod decisively. *Then that's me. I'm the protag . . .
that one.*

The cat smirks, whiskers askew. *I said USUALLY,
dog.*

"LUNA!"

Beatrice stops short, grabs Amelia's wrist. "Did you
hear that?"

"Bea?" a woman's voice calls.

"Amelia, where are you?"

Amelia nods.

Caleb scans the area. "The Driskill hotel—duck in
here!" There are a handful of steps nearby, and he takes
them in one long stride. He pulls open the wood-and-
glass door, and the four of us—minus Sandpaper, who
has disappeared—dash inside.

It's fancy, with glittering lights and colorful glass
art hanging on the ceiling. The marble floors are slick
and cool under my paw pads. The kids tuck behind a
large leather couch, crouch low like small pups in tall
grass. From the sidewalk, we are invisible. Their hearts
pound like the plastic drums we heard earlier. Beatrice
grabs Amelia's hand. It's a sweaty grasp, I can smell,
but Amelia doesn't seem to mind.

Tessa and the other adults pause on the sidewalk

outside. They are only a few leaps away, but on the other side of a thick wall. I don't think my young humans with their tiny, ineffective ears can hear their talk.

Worry sears Tessa around her edges like a slow-burning, smoky fire. "I just can't believe they left."

"Oh, I can. Have you met my Beatrice?"

"You're going to be in a lot of trouble for this, Ms. Greene." This is the man's voice from earlier. Caleb's father. "I am definitely going to report you to the state board for this. What a bunch of attention-seeking kids."

I can feel the tears that sting Tessa's eyes from here. But her emotions are a swirl of dark paint, a mix of blues and greens and purples and blacks, like Amelia's art from last week. A bomb. I can feel her frustration at this man, who will get her in trouble even though she was just trying to get him to stop yelling in front of her kids. I can feel her sadness that she doesn't know where her clients are. I can feel her disappointment in herself.

I peek over the top of the couch. Maybe if Tessa sees me . . .

Tessa nods. Wrings her hands. "Yes, I suppose you should report me. I'll let my mentor know too, of course. I imagine I'll lose my license over this."

Oh.

OH!

66

Lose her license.

That's just as bad—worse!—than me losing all my therapy dog points. Tessa won't be able to counsel people anymore if she loses her license. Tessa's whole heart, her whole light—every bit of her spirit, every bit of her music—goes to her clients.

Counseling is *her* duty.

"But one thing you should know, sir," Tessa continues, "is that these kids aren't seeking attention. They're seeking nurturing."

I'm not certain what that word means, *nurturing*, but it sounds like a cup of warm milk. And it makes this group of adults fall silent.

The kids don't hear any of this, I can tell, because they're busy whispering and hissing at one another, using hand signals to show that they can cut through this fancy hotel, up a flight of stairs, and out the back entrance onto Seventh Street. They would give themselves up if they knew Tessa's career was dangling overhead like raw meat, about to be gobbled by a beast. But they don't know.

"Hang on, folks, my cell phone says Amelia is very close to here," her father's voice says. "I think we've almost caught up to them."

They twist and turn on the street. "Amelia?" "Bea!

Where are you?" "Luna!"

I could trot out there right now. I could bark—heaven forbid I draw that kind of attention to myself while working—and tell them where we are. I could lead the kids back to the church—it'd be easy, with our scent trails—and we could pretend none of this ever happened.

I knew this one pup in training: Freckles. Nice kid. But he soiled himself during class. Soiled himself! I never saw him again. So if that's all it takes to disqualify a dog, I can only imagine what today's hijinks will get me.

But I'm still wearing my bandanna. And when I'm wearing my bandanna, I belong to these kids, not Tessa.

And and? These kids? They're smiling. Snickering. *Talking.*

Their Knots are looser, their Water rushes more gently, their Shadows are easier to spot.

They're becoming a team, just as Tessa hoped. Hope is a star, orienting our spirit. Tessa says that sometimes. When she says stuff like that? It's how you know she is *not* a bad guy.

The kids stay low, quiet, and they whisper, "Luna!" They motion me to follow them up a fancy set of stairs.

They want me to go with them!

I'm a part of this team. I belong to these kids.

So I crouch low too. And I sneak. One paw, then another.

We wind up the wide, marble stairs, into and through a long, wooden room carpeted in stars . . .

. . . and out the back door.

Again.

★ 10 ★

A TEETH MOMENT

The hotel was quiet and cool. The street is loud and hot. It's like being shoved, walking through the swinging door back into this blasty hot noise. My eyes squint. We swing around the corner and trot down a hill. A lady zips by on a scooter wearing high heels and a large necklace. A car spews foul smoke like a dragon, music grumbling from its duct-taped windows. A man passing us mumbles, "Put your dog on a leash. Jeez." The city swirls with all kinds of emotion and energy, and I have to pant to filter through them all. It feels like one large *Go!* and I really prefer *Stay!* It makes my stomach cramp.

Oh!

I pause.

Turn.

Sniff.

I have to *go* too, I realize, and I am surrounded by hot concrete. That will never do for doo. There are a handful of trees on this street, but they are rooted in metal bases. I sniff each one as we pass. Cigarette butts. Dumped-out coffee. Dog pee galore. I wish I could stay and explore these glorious smells, but my kids are on the move.

Caleb must notice my search for the perfect poo spot because he says, "Luna has to relieve herself. Let's go to that park down there." He points to a small patch of grass, a tiny ring of trees farther down the hill. They push a button on a pole—*beep!*—and we wait. Then we cross, passing rows of sun-hot cars, like teeth lined up in a growl. The road is hotter than the sidewalk, and I have to pick up my feet extra high.

We arrive at the grass—*ahhhh*. It's cool and squishy under my paws, and it's times like this that I don't understand why humans wear those foot prisons all the time. *Shoes*, they call them. So hot and stinky. Their toes could be sinking into this cool mud right now.

Grandma trees sway inside this tiny park. *Grandmas*, because these trees are old and wrinkly and their arms droop. These trees have lifted a lot of leaves over the years. They stoop now because of it.

I lower my nose into the tickly grass and *sniiiifffff*. No, that's not the right spot. I move two hops to the left, sniff. No. I spin, sniff. No. I rotate, sniff. No. I am one hop away. Sniff. One shuffle. Sniff. One turn . . .

THERE!

The perfect spot.

Ahhhhhh.

When I finish, I scratch the grass, flinging my scent all about for the benefit of the other dogs. They'll want to sniff that. *You are welcome, fellow canines!*

I wait.

Ahem, I cough politely. *The plastic baggie?*

But instead Beatrice flings the back of her hand against Caleb's chest. "How'd you know Luna had to go to the bathroom? You got a dog?"

Caleb shrugs. We, Caleb and I, feel mildly proud that Beatrice is impressed. "No, I'm allergic. To cats too. But I've done a lot of reading about therapy dogs. My dad says dogs in therapy are nonsense, so I looked it up."

Nonsense. I lift my chin. It has the word *sense* in it, which reminds me of training. Of duty. *I am nonsense*, I repeat.

Sandpaper spits out some of the water he was drinking from a mud puddle. He's back. I thought I'd ditched that mangy cat cutting through the hotel, but no such luck.

Caleb continues, "Luna here has had quite a bit of training. She won't go to the bathroom where she isn't supposed to. That's why we had to come to this park."

I lift my chin a bit, wag my tail slowly. Amelia strokes the top of my head. But no one whips out the plastic baggie, and my poo is just *sitting there*.

"What kinds of training?" Bea asks.

Caleb tugs at the neck of his bloody T-shirt again. He'd crawl out of it if he could. "Well, she has to come when she's called, and she knows commands like *sit* and *stay*, stuff like that. She has to be calm and low-key around all sorts of people and dogs and situations."

I would not be more surprised if I had gum stuck in my fur. I had no idea Caleb knew this much about me and my work. He always seemed as aloof as a cat to me.

Bea cracks her knuckles, grins at me. "That sounds like our Luna."

Our Luna.

I knew they'd come around.

All these smiles about my hard work, my training, make me feel as proud as a poodle on grooming day. I grin back, my tongue lolling out of my mouth. But I'm getting a little jittery because *where is the plastic baggie*?! We are wild as wolves if no one bothers to clean up my business. I don't care for the feeling of being wild as wolves.

"Your dad thinks therapy dogs are nonsense?" Bea pulls on this talk a little more. A Knot can pull things like that.

Nonsense must mean *awesome*, because that's what therapy dogs are.

"Yes. But to be fair, my dad thinks most things are nonsense."

Bea snorts, wheels about, and smacks Caleb on the back. "I like you, dude."

But Caleb isn't quite done. He's rather enjoying this moment of both pleasing Bea and resisting his father. "Therapy dogs offer comfort, reduce anxiety, and reduce aggressive behavior. They're kinda like super-heroes."

Superheroes? I don't know what that means, exactly, but the way Caleb says it, it feels like the ultimate *Who's a Good Dog?*

Bea smiles. "Offer comfort," she says, pointing to Amelia. "Reduce anxiety." Her point swerves to Caleb. "And reduce aggressive behavior." She pounds on her chest. Caleb chuckles; Amelia beams and nods.

I glow like the moon itself. I knew these kids loved me, sure, but I never knew how much they appreciated me. My job. My work. My duty. I'm feeling all waggy and drooly and bursting with moonbeams of love and pride when out of nowhere, a purply sheen swoops right down in front of me, *cacawwwww*!

There are moments where we pause, when we're able to breathe in, breathe out before we make a choice. Then there are moments when—*snap!*—our teeth bite before we even realize our mouths are stretching open.

This was a teeth moment.

I leap, my jaws wrapping around the pigeon. We hang there in midair, it seems, the pigeon and I, while I hear a sickening crack.

I feel it too. The crack. In my bones I feel it.

"Luna, NO!" Beatrice and Caleb both shout.

My feet sink back into the soft earth.

I lay the flapping bird in the tall grass. It does not fly away.

The kids all stare at it, silence filling this space where smiles just were. They all turn to me, the shock on their faces spelling it out: *Luna is a bad dog.*

Their feelings for me swung that fast.

In the flash of a wing, I abandoned all I've been trained to do, my duty. I obeyed instinct instead. How could I act so untamed?

I tuck my tail. Hang my head.

The bird flaps in the grass.

Our souls all whimper like lonely puppies.

I didn't mean to, I say. *I didn't! I promise! I don't know what happened!*

A whine jumbles around in my throat. I droop; I can't make eye contact with these humans.

Every protagonist has a fatal flaw, says a voice from behind a tire of a nearby taco truck. Sandpaper. *It seems our protagonist, Luna, has instincts she cannot control. This does not look good for our Merry Band of Five, friends.*

Shut up, cat, I growl. *And it's FOUR! Merry Band of FOUR!* Another mistake. My trio of kids assume my growling is for this bird. I switch back to whining.

Every protagonist feels misunderstood, Luna, Sandpaper says.

Misunderstood, I echo as the kids furrow their brows at me, the lines of their faces twisting from shock into disgust. At *me.* Being misunderstood feels like being let outside, then being forgotten. Alone and scratching at the door. I feel sick.

Do not worry about being misunderstood, Sandpaper purrs, slinking down the hill toward the lake. *Worry about understanding.*

Worry about understanding? I yell. *All I do is try to understand!* That cat knows nothing about me. It's my job to understand these humans! My duty! I am their moon!

My teeth itch with anger at that cat. With anger at myself. With anger at that stupid bird, swooping too close to my head. With anger . . . yes. At my kids. For not understanding this was *instinct*, not intent. I am a silver Labrador retriever. I was bred to capture birds. Why don't they see that? Why is this any different from Bea's punch? Than Amelia and Caleb and Bea hiding from people who love them?

This is a teeth moment.

★ 11 ★

ODD NUMBERS AND ODD THINGS AND CHESS

D own Congress," Caleb says, pointing downhill toward the shimmery lake. "And then right. That's what the map says."

"No, listen," Beatrice says. "There are bike trails on the other side of the bridge. Let's take those to Zilker. It'd be harder for them"—she jerks her head backward, over her shoulder—"to find us that way."

Caleb is biting his lip, biting back an argument about time and slices of seconds, but Amelia smiles. Nods.

We walk, the hill pulling us. Slowly. Silently.

"Go back, Luna," Beatrice says. After the pigeon they want me to leave again. I won't. But my antics with the bird hang as low and gray as the storm clouds that smear the horizon. I lost sight of my duty, lost my training, and gave in to instinct. I feel *shame*. It is as thick as sickness.

"One, two, three . . ." Caleb mutters. He touches each tree as we pass it, fingertips trailing over bark.

We approach the bottom of the hill. Behind us is the pink dome of the capitol building. In front of us is a long stretch of bridge over the lake.

". . . five, six . . ." It's the only sound any of us make, Caleb's counting.

". . . eight." Caleb stops next to this last tree at the base of the hill. He feels—*we* feel—a sudden, heavy *disappointment*, like finding there are no more dog treats after doing a spectacular trick.

Caleb bites his lip, looks up the hill toward the capitol. *Hesitation* hangs over him.

"C'mon," Beatrice says. "Walk sign. We gotta keep moving."

Caleb swallows, tugs at the neck of his T-shirt. "But there are eight trees."

Beatrice throws her head back, huffs. She is as *impatient* as a squeaky toy. "There are more than eight trees, Caleb. Let's bolt."

Caleb closes his eyes. Breathes deeply. He's trying the calming techniques Tessa taught him. I mirror him:

breathe in, breathe out . . . nice work.

"I wish I had my backpack . . ." he mutters. I feel him miss the goo he slathers on his hands. He's touched trees and he doesn't have it.

Ah, our seeker from the House of Caleb faces an obstacle. It's Sandpaper again, his cat voice sliding out from behind a metal pole. The walk sign beeps loudly, noting that the time to cross the street is closing. *This is exactly what our quest requires.*

I roll my eyes. *Hush, cat. He's working through something.*

Indeed! Aren't we all?

Are we?

Beatrice cracks her knuckles, bounces on her toes. Her eyes land on Sandpaper, but before she can finish saying, "Hey, kitty!" Sandpaper has vanished behind a bike rack. The sign flashes a "Don't Walk" red hand. "Okay," she says to Caleb. "Tell me. Eight trees?"

Caleb sizzles like a sparkler, burning with embarrassment. "Yes. Between here and the park we left. And well . . . that's a problem."

"It's a problem," Beatrice repeats. Her flannel shirt is knotted around her waist, and she tugs at the arms. "Because . . . ?"

"It's unnatural."

Beatrice mashes her lips, and like she often does,

she crackles with a mixture of feelings: Amusement. Impatience. Curiosity. I love how beautifully a Knot can fray. "Go on."

Caleb looks pained, like he has a sore tooth. "Well, eight trees, so perfectly spaced like this . . . that would never occur in nature. It's unnatural."

Our seeker is correct, Sandpaper says, dusty whiskers poking from behind a bike tire. *Eight trees. It would not occur. I like his sensibilities.*

You can't count that high, I quip to the cat, largely because I can't count that high, and I can't imagine a cat doing anything I can't do.

"Odd numbers occur in nature," Caleb says, yanking at the hem of his T-shirt, then the neck again. He unbuttons a button on his outer, crisper shirt. "Like pi. And the zeros and ones in computer code. And Fibonacci spirals."

Ah yes, those, Sandpaper says, nodding knowingly, as if he knows exactly what a . . . a Fibbing spiral is.

Beatrice scratches her chin. "So you're obsessed with things being imperfect? Because this is the right crowd for you, bud."

Caleb actually manages a chuckle through his distress, and it's like watching an egg crack. There's a strange beauty inside an egg.

"I'm obsessed with things being natural," he says.

Bea nods slowly. "And an odd number of trees would do that. Make it look natural."

Caleb beams with being understood at last, and I feel it too: it's like the thrill of hope that goes with a human holding up a leash. "Yes! Exactly!"

"Pretty sure it's still unnatural if you're planning for it to look natural," Bea says gently. She's tiptoeing into Caleb's world of ideas.

Caleb sighs. Nods. "I know. That's very upsetting, don't you think?"

Beatrice tiptoes further. "Well, eight. It's like eight pawns on a chessboard, right? And there are eight trees lining the other side of the street. So that's pretty cool, isn't it? Like they're facing off?"

Caleb blinks. "You know chess?"

Beatrice arches an eyebrow at him. The pink bun on the top of her head slides around cockily as she plants a fist on her hip. "Yes, I know chess."

The sign beeps, telling us to walk. And Caleb does it: he walks, because this girl understands odd numbers and odd things and chess.

The street is hot but cooling. Steamy, still, hours after the last rain. Four of us stride through the painted white crosswalk.

I pause. Sniff the air.

Panic makes my heart leap like a frog. *Nonono-nono . . .*

I was worried about Caleb, about his obsessions, and I didn't see. I didn't *feel* it!

Sandpaper grins with a twitch of his whiskers and narrates: *Luna notices that she seems to have misplaced something.*

As soon as Sandpaper says it, Beatrice stops too.

"Where's Amelia?!"

★ 12 ★

A WHOLE DICTIONARY
OF HUGS

A MELIA?!" Caleb shouts. His voice cracks, a pup's yip becoming a big dog's bark.

"Shhhhh!" Beatrice says, her green eyes sliding around the area. Crowds now clog the bridge we're about to cross. There are lots of ankles and knees and jeans and boots and sandals planted on the sidewalk as these humans overlook the water below. "You don't want our parents to hear, do you? They can't be far behind."

See, Sandpaper says. *Antagonists. Bad guys.*

They aren't bad guys! I snap. I sniff the crowd. *AMELIA?!*

We—Beatrice, Caleb, Sandpaper, and I—weave

through the crowds whispering, "Amelia?" "Where are you, Amelia?"

Luna begins to panic as she realizes she's lost one of her charges, Sandpaper narrates.

I narrow my eyes at that cat. *Not panic*, I say, though that's exactly what I feel. *Panic* feels like having your ball sail over a too-high fence. A favorite thing, gone as you watch.

I am failing at my duty.

This bridge is hot. It bakes all day in the sun and there are no trees to hug it with shade. I pant.

I bump into a knee here, step on a sandaled foot there. I look up. Above me hover hundreds of bellies and chins and nostrils. This crowd is dizzying and confusing and it smells like hot summer feet. "Dude. Put your dog on a leash," a bearded fellow growls. I growl back.

I miss my routine. My row of quiet habits. I miss *Amelia*.

And here, in this crowd, it is so difficult to sort out my kids' feelings from everyone else's. It's like walking through mud, there are so many emotions hanging in the air. Desperation. Wonder. Grief. Glee.

Beatrice and Caleb sweat. Their hearts race. Their eyes scan the crowd. Beatrice drums her knuckles on the metal railing too hard; it *pings* like a loud bell and she winces.

85

But Caleb is tall. "There!" he shout-whispers, and points his long, lanky finger at a girl. At Amelia.

We weave through more knees, over more toes, and we reach her. Amelia leans over the metal rail, her sundress billowing in the wind, her pile of ropey hair shining in the orange sun. She's looking at her blue screen. She's so calm, and we are so worried. She's simply wandered off, it appears. A Shadow, stretching farther as the sun lowers.

My heart sings but Beatrice's snarls. She grabs Amelia's shoulders, spins her so they are face-to-face.

"Don't do that!" Beatrice shouts, breaking her own don't-shout-because-the-parents-might-hear rule. "You can't *ever* do that, you hear? If you're not going to talk to us, you can't just wander away like that, because then we can't find you. Got it?"

The Merry Band of Five has an internal conflict, as each group must, Sandpaper quips.

Beatrice's hands are still on Amelia's shoulders. Her chest heaves like she's just run as far and fast as the wind. She's shaking. She is perhaps the desperation I smelled earlier.

Amelia's eyelashes flutter. Her eyes get glassy and salty. And shaking must be contagious, because Amelia starts shaking too. She nods, then flings her arms around Beatrice's waist in a tight hug. Beatrice pauses, then hugs her back.

Our fair seekers have overcome another obstacle in their quest, Sandpaper says. *They are proving themselves quite worthy of their task.*

Amelia and Beatrice stand there like that, hugging, for a long time. I feel like I should wag my tail because *hugs!* but this feels different. This feels like an *I'm sorry* hug, rather than an *I love you* hug. Who knew there is a whole dictionary of hugs? I usually only get the one.

Caleb shifts on his large galumphy feet. "I'm glad we found you, Amelia."

This breaks apart the *I'm sorry* hug. Amelia sniffs, lightly swipes at her cheeks. She turns her blue screen toward Beatrice and Caleb.

Beatrice squints at it. "The map?"

Amelia shrugs. She points at a flashing blue dot on the screen. Caleb clucks.

"I get it," he says. "Your dad. He's tracking us using your cell."

Amelia nods.

Beatrice looks from Caleb to Amelia, her fists knotting. "Yeah? Okay. Maybe we should ditch your phone then, A. You know, until—"

But before Beatrice can finish her thought, Amelia

turns and chucks her phone over the metal railing. It sails through the orange sunset air in a slow arc, falling, falling. The water is so far below, the splash sounds like a tiny sink drip. I doubt these humans can even hear it.

Plip!

The trio of kids is silent.

Ah, a plot twist this narrator did not see coming! Sandpaper says, tail twitching with delight. *Our Merry Band of Five removes itself further from the outside world. It is all going according to literary canon!*

FOUR, I stress. *Band of FOUR.*

"Dang, girl," Beatrice breathes, looking over the rail at the growing white ring where the phone hit the water. "I just meant we should maybe hide the thing until we could come back later and get it. You don't do anything halfway, do you?"

Amelia giggles through tears. Another rainbow. We've seen a lot of those today.

"And that," Caleb says, still looking at the white ring sinking phones make, "was our map to Zilker." He puffs his cheeks. Looks at his watch. Mutters, "Seven twenty-five . . ." Caleb feels *conflicted*, my whiskers tell me. *Conflicted* is a bit like playing tug-of-war, but only with yourself. Which is no fun.

The panic I felt just a moment ago—a sailing arc of a tennis ball over a too-tall fence—burbles up again after watching that sailing arc of a cell phone hit the water. I don't know much about humans and their screens, but I know they rely on them *a lot*. For directions and seeking food and talking to loved ones. Humans feel safety when they clutch their screens; screens are a dependable, warm blanket. What will we do without one?

Should I turn these kids around now? Lead them back to the church? Follow our scents home and face our punishments?

I should. I—

Scccreeeeee! Scrriiiiittcchh! Screeaaaattchh!

A chorus of high-pitched wails pulses out from underneath the bridge we're standing on. It sounds like sirens. No, not sirens. The sound—it's higher than that. It sounds like balloons rubbing against each other. Like Styrofoam squeaking in tight boxes. Like chalk on a sidewalk. I can feel these screeches in every hair of my fur, in every tooth, in my toenails. My head cocks one way, then the other. My silver ears flop.

Sandpaper chuckles at my apparent confusion. He licks his lips. *Here is where things get interesting, friends. A temptation to stray from our quest. Our very own siren song. Because lo and behold: here come the bats.*

★ 13 ★

HERE COME THE BATS

It begins as a pulse of noise, but so high-pitched, it's likely these humans *feel* it rather than hear it, like being wrapped inside a heartbeat. The hum throbs out from the bridge beneath our feet, rising and vibrating, a silver shimmer of sound wavering across the orange sunset sky.

The smell is next. The stirring of millions of creatures unfurling wings, uncurling toes. It causes a waft of scent to rise to our nostrils. It's a wild animal smell— musky and earthy. But with a tinge of guano—bat poo.

And then they pour out of the small holes carved beneath this bridge, these bats. One by one, but by the thousands. They pour and they pour and they pour, black ink spilled onto an orange sky. They lift and they swirl, they stretch thin and they cloud together. Moving, pulsing, swaying. Thousands become one.

The bats are the opposite of nighttime: instead of orange dots on a black sky, here are black dots on an orange sky. *Alive.* Like changing constellations from a too-rapidly spinning earth, each bat a star. Tessa likes to look up at the stars and point out the pictures the constellations make: Orion, Pegasus, Leo, Draco. I wag when she does this, because while I can't really see the pictures she traces with her delicate fingertip, it makes her happy. But here! These bats lift into a volcano, whirl into a dragon, stretch into a curling snake. I watch this, and I wonder: Do humans see pictures in their heads too?

"Wow," Beatrice breathes. "I've heard about this, but I've never seen it."

Caleb nods once. "One-point-five million Mexican free-tailed bats."

Bats pull the sky toward them. They climb awkwardly, with great vigor and much flapping. Birds sail like sleek needles over silk, but bats earn every inch of height they gain.

People all around lift their cameras, their screens, and record the masterpiece these bats paint for us. We're hidden from the approaching adults inside this crowd. It's hard to be here, though. It's one thing to sort out my humans' feelings from the noises in the city: sirens and horns and engines. It's another here, on this bridge, with all these people. It's so heavy with mood. I'm surprised this bridge doesn't collapse.

"A group of bats is called a colony, but it's sometimes called a cloud. Appropriate, isn't it?" Caleb says as we watch a more than million bats etch the sky.

Beatrice never takes her eyes off the bats, but she smirks. "You don't know." She's teasing, I believe. Beatrice walks a fine line between teasing and shoving.

Caleb mashes his lips to hold in a grin. "A group of owls is called a parliament. A group of hawks is called a kettle. A group of butterflies is called a kaleidoscope."

Beatrice folds her arms over her chest, breaking the spell by looking away from the bats and at Caleb. "A group of Calebs is called a smart aleck."

She means it to be funny, I can tell by her arched eyebrow. But Caleb falls silent. He turns and allows himself to be hypnotized by the bats again. He is stung.

Beatrice feels—*we* feel—confused and hurt by this. Weren't we playing? Isn't that how friends act? Don't they give each other a hard time? Our hurt blazes slowly into smoky fury. Beatrice grits her teeth, knots her fists. She takes the toe of her boot and kicks the metal rail *ping ping ping*. "Wake up, bats!" she shouts. "Wakey, wakey!"

The people around us shift away, like they smell a fart. They were just enjoying this mesmerizing sight, and here's this kid, causing a scene. Caleb folds his long arms over his chest. Amelia edges her chin away from us ever so slightly. We feel *frustrated* with Beatrice right now.

It's how they felt about me, hurting that bird.

This is Beatrice's instinct, this tightness. This kicking.

Ah, more challenges arise for our Merry Band of Five, Sandpaper purrs next to me. He's licking a dirty orange paw, drawing it casually over his ear. *A riff between the main characters, it seems. This makes our quest all the more interesting, does it not? In past times they would duel to the death.*

FOUR, I snap. *And why are you here?* Sandpaper ignores the question. I wish I could ignore things the way a cat can ignore things.

I shake my head, jangle my tags. This is all so new to me, this huge world out here. Our feelings have to be so BIG to get noticed in all this space, all this noise. I blink at the haze of bats still somehow pouring out of this bridge, each individual bat including themselves in the cloud. It's what emotions feel like to me, I realize. Each feeling is individual, but it blends with others to form shapes and sizes. Some round and swooping and graceful; others pointy and sharp and foreboding. And each feeling, when added to a bigger swirl of other feelings, gets amplified. It's hard. It would be easier if it were bat by bat.

I whimper a bit, thinking of how overwhelming it can be, all these strong feelings, hacking and punching and pushing one another. Beatrice hears my whine. She stops kicking, stoops, and flings her arms around my neck.

"Thank you for coming with us, Luna," she whispers into the soft fold of my ear. She squeezes my neck. "I kinda didn't want you here, but I need you here."

She sees my duty! Her heart hugs mine, and I give her a quick lick on the chin. She tastes like confusion. She wrinkles her nose and nuzzles me.

The bats squeak and pulse and loom overhead. It seems Beatrice feels my heart because she takes a wavery breath and says, "It's hard to see just one bat, isn't it?"

Amelia tilts her chin back to the two of us, nods. Caleb's grip on his own arms loosens a bit, his Waterfall shifting ever so slightly. "It is."

Sandpaper coughs a tiny guffaw. *Was Luna's well-timed sob a clever move, or just dumb luck? Let's see if our protagonist can hold this Merry Band of Five together to the climax of our tale, shall we? When at last we'll see our true hero emerge.*

Dumb luck is better than no luck, cat, I say, and I give Beatrice another quick kiss. *And it's FOUR.*

"Hey, there's that cat again," Beatrice says, loosening her grip on my neck. "Here, kitty kitty!" She leans over, still squatting, but Sandpaper is too quick. Just a whip of a tail and *snap!* He's lost in the crowd.

The moving crowd. Because the spill of bats, while still going, is now thinning. The people are moving on to the next miracle.

A kid on a scooter whizzes by, and Beatrice has to fling herself backward from her squat so her fingers don't get run over. "Hey!" she shouts in his wake. Her knuckles scrape the sidewalk, eating pebbles. Her head whacks the metal rail.

Caleb and Amelia rush to help Beatrice stand. "Are you okay?" Caleb asks. Amelia squeezes Bea's hand, checks out her skinned knuckles.

Beatrice dusts herself off. Rubs the back of her head. She feels grumbly like gravel, but when she sees the concerned tilt of Caleb's eyes, feels the attention from Amelia, she softens like sand. "Yeah. What a *mumble-hole.*"

I don't understand the word Beatrice uses, but it

makes Amelia titter behind her hand.

Caleb blinks. Swallows. "My mother says there is always a better way to express yourself than using a curse word."

"Better than calling that dude a *mumble*hole? I don't think so."

Amelia is laughing outright now, like bright dandelions popping up from fresh green grass. But Caleb reddens. Shifts. Tugs at the bloody neck of his T-shirt.

Beatrice must pick up on how uncomfortable Caleb is, and here's one thing I've noticed: humans are usually *great* at knowing how other humans feel. But their own feelings get in the way of them knowing what to do next. Tessa has these magnets that she uses sometimes in counseling sessions; she says the two ends that are alike actually push each other away. Humans do that a lot with each other.

"You don't ever cuss?" Beatrice asks Caleb.

"Oh, sure, I do," Caleb stammers. He works his jaw. "We should, you know. Get moving . . ."

"You don't," Beatrice says. "But you should. It'd make you feel better. Loosen you up."

"I don't need to be loosened."

"Au contraire, *mon frère*," Beatrice says. "I think you do." And I find this funny because Beatrice is the

Knot here. Loosening is something she works on all the time.

"Shout one out now," Beatrice continues. She waves her skinned hand over the side of the bridge. The sky is now turning lilac at the edges, the lights of the city beginning to bounce off the green-brown water.

"I . . . don't know. We should get going. Hector will only be at the park until nine. And our parents . . ." Caleb stands on tiptoes, looking over the thinning crowd. "We should go."

"Cay-*leeeeb*," Beatrice sings. She pokes at him with both pointer fingers and bounces on her toes. "C'mon, Caleb . . ."

"Beatrice!" Caleb snaps. Beatrice leaps backward like she's seen a snake. Caleb's brow tightens. My brow tightens.

"We should *go*."

Here's the thing. Caleb is a Waterfall. If he wants to say no, he will. He will plow forward relentlessly. But this isn't a no, and Beatrice knows it. And Beatrice understands *relentless*. They can both be bloodhounds.

Beatrice lets the *should* part of Caleb's comment hang in the air for an extra heartbeat. Then she begins again, gentler.

"C'mon . . ." Beatrice elbows him, rubs her skinned

knuckles. "Real quick. Shout out the foulest, stinkiest word you know. Then we'll go."

Caleb huffs, rolls his eyes, then nods once. His face shifts. He steps up to the railing, grips the metal, and clears his throat. His frustration melts into nervous excitement, here on the edge.

Caleb breathes in deepdeepdeep, and bellows:

"CHECKMAAAAAAAAAATE!"

He stands there, wavering. His shoulders drop. He beams.

He turns to Beatrice. "Let's go."

But Beatrice now blinks. That is rare. "Did you just shout . . . *checkmate*?"

Amelia mashes her lips, unsure whether or not to giggle.

"I did. And you were right. That felt great. Thanks, Beatrice."

"But"—Beatrice adjusts the flannel shirt tied at her waist—"that's not a cuss word."

"You didn't tell me to shout a cuss word," Caleb says. His eyes are shining. Glee, not glum. "You told me to shout the foulest, stinkiest word I know. And that's *checkmate*."

Amelia does it. She giggles.

"Checkmate," Beatrice repeats. "That's the foulest word you know."

Caleb beams, and it's like watching light glitter through the mist of a Waterfall. "Absolutely! It means death and destruction! It means bloody battles and coldhearted strategy and terrifying defeat and kingdoms falling! It's the deterioration of a whole society! A regime is about to crumble! The world as you know it will cease to be! If that's not foul and stinky, I don't know what is!" Caleb is fully satisfied. He lifts his chin, and I realize I can't think of the last time I saw that particular slant of his jaw. It's usually tucked into his chest.

Beatrice shifts. Here she was, trying to unloosen Caleb, and she's the one slackening. She steps up to the rail.

"CHECKMAAAAAAAAAAATE!"

A man with a bushy gray beard who totters by rolls his eyes. *"Kids."*

These kids—*my* kids—laugh. Together. Caleb and Beatrice head to the opposite side of the bridge.

But Amelia hasn't had a turn. She steps up on the bottom rail, cowboy-boot toes wedged between metal slats. She leans too far over. My heart leaps into my throat. This bridge is HIGH and the water below is LOW. Beatrice and Caleb both freeze. She is stretched dangerously thin, this Shadow.

Amelia screams, "AHHHHHHHHHHHHHHHHH!"

She is red-faced. She trembles. Tendrils of hair shake

loose from her ropey braids. But she keeps screaming.

"AHHHHHHHHHHHHHHHH!"

And then she is done.

I've never heard her voice before. It is stronger, more powerful than I imagined. Like a song inside a scream.

She hops backward off the rail and dusts her hands. She jerks her head toward the opposite side of the bridge and marches toward it.

"Well, I'll be checkmated," Beatrice mutters. Caleb chuckles.

Beatrice links her elbow through Caleb's, and he doesn't recoil.

They follow Amelia.

They're off to find Hector.

He is their *quest*.

I follow them.

They are my *quest*.

★ 14 ★

VOTE: BORROW OR STARVE

Beatrice's stomach grumbles as they descend the opposite side of the bridge. "I'm hungry," she says. "This is usually when my mom and I eat dinner."

Caleb nods. "That's wise, to get something to eat now. The trail to Zilker Park probably won't have anywhere to stop for food or water. I think there's a convenience store a block or so up."

He pauses, looks at that wrist-collar of his. "But we need to hurry, you know? It's already seven forty-five. We've still got about . . . mmm . . . two miles, I think? We can make two miles in an hour, but—"

Beatrice waves her hand like she's swatting away a pesky fly. "Plenty of time."

Caleb's forehead creases. "It's not. But we do have time to eat."

They climb the hill, now on the opposite side of the lake from our church. From home. It's the soft purple part of the day but it's still very hot. I pant; these kids sweat. It's the part of summer when summer has lasted too long, blazed too bright, and you can't remember what *cold* feels like. The leaves are crisping around their edges, but they haven't yet whispered goodbye to their trees. Everything is thirsty.

It appears we are now going to a *convenience store*, whatever that is. No one actually says, "Let's go there," or "We can get food from that place." Here's the thing: humans are really good at filling in the blanks when it comes to words. They sometimes don't complete their sentences, the rest of their words stolen by the wind. They sometimes don't even use words, but instead bob their heads or point their fingers or shrug their shoulders. It can all be very confusing to a dog. Why don't humans always talk since they can? I'd talk nonstop if I could. And how are humans so good at hearing words that aren't there, but so bad at listening to feelings that definitely are?

There is a neon-white building buzzing at the top of the hill, and we approach it. Cars zoom in and out, and the air smells like exhaust and gasoline. As we get close, the doors slide open like a magic trick. Caleb turns to me.

"Sit, Luna," he says. He even uses the hand gesture for *sit*: a cupped palm. He's been paying closer attention to Tessa than I realized. "Stay." He shows me his palm, like a *stop* signal.

I plop my booty on the hot sidewalk and whimper as Amelia slides through the magic doors. They're going in without me?

Beatrice scowls. "What are you doing?" I grumble to match Beatrice's question.

Caleb points to a sticker on the magic door, a dog behind a circle and a line. But I don't look anything like the dog on that sticker. That dog looks like Zeus, this diabetic alert dog I once met, all pointy ears and long bushy tail. This store doesn't want Zeus inside, but they don't say anything about Luna. "No animals allowed."

Beatrice folds her arms over her chest. "Luna doesn't have to stay out here. She's a service dog. They can go anywhere."

My tail droops to the hot sidewalk. I skootch a bit more toward the door. *Technically, I'm not a service dog.*

"Technically, she's not a service dog," Caleb echoes. "She's a therapy animal. Federal laws don't grant therapy dogs the same access as a service—"

"Oh, hush," Beatrice says. She tugs on my collar. "These store people don't know that! Move, Luna!"

Caleb sighs. "The correct command is *come, Luna*."

"Come, Luna!"

I glance at Caleb, but he's not that worried about winning this fight. So I walk inside the convenience store behind Beatrice. The doors *heesh* open with a giant dragon hiss, and I jump.

The floor is sticky-grungy and cold and it ticks under my toenails. The too-white lights remind me of the horrid church basement; they hum and flicker and pop. It's cold in here, compared to the warm Texas evening outside. But the smells! Hot dogs that spin inside a glass case. Some kind of meat wrapped in corn husks. Popcorn!

Beatrice unties the flannel shirt around her waist and puts it on over her arms. She and Caleb and Amelia all grab food: chips and candy, sodas and water. The trio gathers at the back of the store, next to the humming cold closets lined with rows of gem-colored plastic drinks.

"Okay," Beatrice whispers. "Here's the plan. Gimme your stash. I can cram some of the food in my cargo shorts and probably in my waistband. My flannel will cover most of the lumps. Caleb, you'll need to cram at least one cold drink in your underwear, capisce?"

"*Stealing?!*" Caleb hiss-whispers. Terror floods through him. It smells like poison.

"Shhhh!" Beatrice's eyes flare. Amelia calmly takes the food cradled in everyone's arms. She walks away.

"We are *not* stealing that food," Caleb loud-whispers, arms folded. Here he is: the Waterfall at full force. There is no containing water once it has made up its mind what it wants. "That's illegal. I thought you had money." His shoulders fall. "My money's in my back-pack. Back at the church you made us leave."

Beatrice rolls her eyes, so I heavy sigh to echo her irritation. Her impatience smells like burnt toast. "I didn't make you go anywhere. And *no*, I don't have money! I never have money! Look. This is one of those ethical situations Tessa is always talking about."

"Ethical situations?" The rush of Caleb's waterfall tapers slightly.

"Yes. Do we borrow a teeny, tiny snack from this neighbor of ours, or do we starve to death and die?"

Now it's Caleb's turn to smell impatient. His impatience smells more like scorched marshmallows. "That's a biased poll. You can't ask the question that way."

"I just did. So on the count of three, vote: borrow or starve. Ready?"

"No, I'm not ready! Jeez. I have all sorts of money in my backpack. Back at the church you made us leave."

"I *didn't* make you leave, and that *doesn't* help us now. Okay. Vote on three. Borrow or starve. One, two . . ."

A loud, two-note whistle cuts the air like scissors. We all swing to look at it. Amelia leans around the corner; a plastic bag full of lumpy things dangles from her wrist. She raises her eyebrows, teasing.

Beatrice blinks, then beams. "You bought our stuff?"

Caleb feels *relief. Relief* is the feeling you have when your human finally comes home after being gone forever, like for six hours or ten minutes. Like finally getting to lick their face after their face has been gone all day. Like peeing.

"Thanks, Amelia," he says. We walk to the front of the store.

"Hey!" a woman wearing glasses that make her look like an insect leans over the counter. "Get that mutt outta here, kids. C'mon!"

I look over my shoulder for a mutt.

"We're going, we're going!" Beatrice snaps. She slides her fingers under my collar. "Come, Luna!"

Me? I'm the mutt?! I feel *anger* bite at my tummy. I feel a growl rolling around inside me like a heavy ball. It feels like instinct rolling over duty.

The woman smacks the counter with her palm when

we pass, and I jump. We duck back through the hissing magic dragon doors. The heat hugs us. Why humans prefer refrigerated rooms to warmth I'll never know.

Amelia rummages around in the bag, doles out goodies. Beatrice unpeels the wrapper off a bar, sinks her teeth in. It's chewy and gooey. "Mmmm. Chocolate. My favorite food group." Caleb nods, takes a bite of something similar.

Chocolate? These kids are eating *poison*! I have to stop them. I paw at Beatrice's boot, but she doesn't notice me. I whine.

Stop eating that! I shout. *You'll have to go to the vet and they'll feed you charcoal to make you throw up on purpose!*

Silly protagonist. Sandpaper's voice comes from across the parking lot. *Chocolate is only bad for dogs.*

I watch the kids. Their eyes roll back in their heads. They were so hungry and now they're so happy. *I . . . I knew that.*

Beatrice shakes up a soda, opens it with a *SPLOOSH!* Caleb takes deep, calming breaths, trying to overlook her messiness. She chugs soda, then *burrr-rrrrps* with gusto.

Caleb's frown deepens.

"What?" Beatrice says with another tiny burp. "It's bubbly."

Amelia rustles in the plastic bag again. She withdraws a long brown stick wrapped in plastic. When she unwraps it, the glorious smell of deeply salted meat tickles my nostrils.

She snaps off a piece of this stick, hands it to me. I inhale it and it is GLORIOUS. Smoky and salty and meaty. Amelia giggles and offers me another pinch of this mystery meat. What is this amazing stick and why aren't I eating it at all times? I drool.

Amelia rustles through the bag once more and digs out a blue plastic pouch. She rips open the top and it smells so fishy it's like a punch in the snout.

Amelia crosses the convenience store parking lot toward Sandpaper. She gently lays the open pouch next to him, at the base of a gas tank. His tail twitches, but he pauses.

Our hero is unsure of these humans' intentions, he narrates.

Ahem, I sniff. *I'M the hero here?*

"Aw, sweet kitty," Beatrice says around a mouthful of drooly chocolate. "Go ahead. Eat!"

Amelia balances on the toes of her cowboy boots. She nudges the tuna packet closer to Sandpaper.

"Go on. Take it, kitty," Beatrice urges from across the lot.

Tuna, Sandpaper purrs, sniffing the pouch. *Protag-onist, can your humans be trusted?*

What? I ask. *Of course! Would I be here if they couldn't be trusted?*

Yes. Dogs are notoriously bad judges of character, Sandpaper says, still smelling the package. *They trust everyone.*

You're the bad judge of character! I say, as frustrated as a stone of kibble stuck between my teeth. *You're the one who can't be trusted!*

Are you suggesting I'm unreliable? Ah, but I do love a good unreliable narrator, Sandpaper says. He licks the tuna out of the pouch. The four of us gather and stand there next to the gas pump, eating and watching this one-eyed cat, just as cats prefer.

A car rumbles up to the tank. It spews black smoke out its backside, and it's painted not-shiny like other cars, but a flat, dull color, like on walls. And someone has painted different-colored shapes all over it: triangles and squares and circles. Sandpaper teeths the pouch of tuna and scurries away.

The humans inside the car tumble out in clumsy glee. They take the hose from the tank and put gasoline in their car. They tip up silvery cans to their lips and put what smells like gasoline in their bellies.

Caleb clears his throat, an attempt to ignore this shuddering, lurching car. He turns to Amelia. "Did you ask the clerk for directions to Zilker?"

Beatrice scoffs around a huge wad of gum. "Of course she didn't. She doesn't *talk*, dude."

Caleb's face shadows pull down. "That's rude."

"What? She doesn't! That's not rude, is it, A?" Beatrice spins, slinging an arm over Amelia's shoulder. "Them's the facts, jack."

Amelia isn't angry. In fact she seems . . . *amused*? *Amused* is what dogs feel when humans coo at them in a high-pitched, squeaky voice.

One of the guys from the car burps loudly. They notice at last we are here. I feel my kids shrink under their gaze. I don't like it.

The driver, a young man in a red hat, crooks a smirk at us. "What are y'all? Scooby and the gang or something?"

His friend spews a laugh while sipping from his silver can. He wears those dark glasses that humans wear in bright sunlight even though the day is now lilac. I don't like it when humans wear glasses like that. It's harder to tell what they're feeling when I can't see their eyes. "Those meddling kids!" They share a sly smile.

Mr. Red Hat tilts his chin up at me. "That your

dog?" He and his friend are older than my kids here but younger than Tessa. Teens.

"Yes," Beatrice and Caleb both answer. Amelia nods. My spirit leaps and sings like a cricket. I'm their dog! But it's a brief cricket song, because my whiskers tell me something is very *off* about these two teens.

The friend of Mr. Red Hat sniffs. "Good hunting dog, I bet."

"Luna doesn't hunt." Beatrice stiffens. She's the Knot. She reaches down and slides her fingers under my collar again. It's a bit too tight. Chokey. I gag.

"Sure she hunts," the red-hat human says. "Dogs'll do whatever we tell 'em to, right, Bryce?"

Mr. Dark Glasses, Bryce, nods slowly. "I'd train that dog to fetch every dove I kill."

And there it is again: the memory of me leaping up, grabbing that pigeon in my jaws. *Snap!* I can feel the image hover over us, a movie in each of our minds. I didn't even know I could do that. I didn't want to. I just . . . did. It's what happens when you let instinct take over. I feel shame: sick and green, like I've eaten too much grass.

How did these people I don't even know make me feel bad about myself?

Dark Glasses Bryce sucks his teeth and leans against

the car. He looks at us in a way that makes me feel like I have the mange. The fur along my spine prickles.

"Hey, I know you!" the teen in the red hat drawls. He leans sideways, looking at Amelia's lowered eyes. His speech is slow and thick in his mouth.

Amelia shakes her head at a grease spot on the parking lot.

Bryce pulls his dark glasses down to the tip of his nose. "Yeah, yeah. You're right, Luke." He pushes himself off his colored-shape car, crosses to her. He reaches toward Amelia's face, but she shrinks away.

"Don't do that," Beatrice says through clenched teeth.

"Nah, listen," Bryce says, fully removing his glasses and hooking them into the collar of his T-shirt. His eyes are red, and he's leaning toward Amelia. "You're that kid whose house burned down. Yeah, a couple blocks from our high school. All the clubs gave y'all clothes and food and stuff. And then you . . . ah, what? Something happened."

"She stopped talking," said Red Hat Teen. He's bouncing on his toes, which I think is odd, this joy about someone who stops talking. "That house was *destroyed*. And the fire department said it was arson. Somebody *started* that fire, man. It wasn't some accident."

Bryce leans in farther. Amelia arches backward from him.

"Cut it out," Caleb squeaks. He has a knot in his throat. We lick our dry lips.

Bryce ignores him. "You still don't talk, huh?" he whispers at Amelia. Something about the way he says it—it's not full of sadness, like a lot of people feel around Amelia. It's not even full of pity. It's full of . . . fascination? And it scares me. The fur on my spine stands taller.

Bryce's eyes narrow. He leans in, over her ear. "You start that fire?" he asks Amelia. She recoils like she's been punched.

"STOP IT!" Beatrice yells. "C'mon, guys." She pulls me by the collar, and it hurts a little. I hack a cough. I'm confused why she doesn't trust me to follow them. Haven't I done that all day?

Bryce snorts, and the red hat guy does too. "Easy, kid," Bryce says, putting his glasses back on. The way he says *kid* to Beatrice, even though he's only a few years older than her, reminds me of Goliath. "No harm, no foul. Y'all need a ride somewhere?" Something about the way he says this makes a new growl roll around in my stomach.

"No," Beatrice and Caleb say again, and Amelia

shakes her head. I realize that all three of them agree when these hair-prickling boys are around. Beatrice tugs me again, too hard.

"Let's *go*," she says. And we leave, but the eyes of those two humans follow us.

★ 15 ★

SURPRISE FEELS LIKE A SNORF OF BLACK PEPPER

Caleb looks over his shoulder a couple of times as we walk toward the trail that will take us to Zilker Park. At least, we *think* it's the trail that'll take us to Zilker Park. We seem less certain now that we don't have a blue screen.

Caleb feels *nervous*. *Nervous* feels like frogs jumping around inside your belly, all slimy and floppy. But after a few steps, when the triangle-painted car stays put at the gas tank and the fellas stay put at the triangle-painted car, his frogs calm a bit. He turns to Amelia.

"You okay?" he says.

Amelia sighs. That is not a yes and not a no. She

burns with embarrassment, and it smells like scorched cocoa. But Amelia's embarrassment isn't tinged with white-hot anger, as I thought it might be. As embarrassment so often is. No, instead it is colored with pink frustration. At herself. Because NO, she doesn't talk. And NO, she doesn't know why. But here's the thing: she didn't need any words to communicate that to me.

Beatrice scowls around a huge wad of gum. "Buncha jerks." She digs into the deep pockets on her shorts, pulls out a chunk of plastic. She beams like she's showing the others a new squeaky toy.

Caleb sees it and flicks his eyes back uphill at the gas station, at the car still sitting by the pump. "Is that their gas cap?"

Beatrice grins like a stretching cat. "Yeah. That old junker of theirs won't get too far without one."

Caleb's brow furrows, and so does mine. Beatrice tosses the plastic cap in a rusty, stinky metal box as we pass it. It clangs against the bottom in a way that makes me cringe.

"I don't think that was a good idea, Bea," Caleb says. "Those guys don't seem like the type to laugh something like that off."

"They don't get to talk to Amelia like that," Beatrice says. She pops her gum like it's a nail getting hammered, like *bam*, we're done discussing it. "So. Are we headed in the right direction for Zilker, Mr. Navigator, sir?"

Amelia digs inside the white plastic bag from the convenience store. She pulls out a thick, folded piece of paper.

"A map! Good idea," Caleb says.

Beatrice grabs the map out of Amelia's hand, unfolds it. It's colorful, with blue lines and red lines and green lines and gray lines. It looks like gibberish, but then, most things that humans put on paper look like gibberish to me.

Beatrice stops. She clutches the open map in her fists, staring at it. I feel her heart skip faster but I don't know why.

Caleb leans over her shoulder. He turns the square map one notch to the left. "It can be easier to read a map like this—"

Beatrice yanks the map out of his hands. The large colorful paper rips.

So does Beatrice.

"I KNOW how to read A MAP!"

Beatrice looks at the ripped map. I feel her anger boil over like pasta on a stove. She rips the map further. Then more. Then again and again and again. Her teeth are tight and her eyes are arrows.

The map is now bits of paper. Beatrice throws them at Caleb and Amelia. I expect it to be forceful and hurtful, but the paper flutters like bits of confetti at a party. The hot wind carries some of it away into the purple sky.

"Do you ever listen to anyone other than yourself?" Caleb snaps. "Gah!" He kicks at a bit of paper near his shoe.

But instead of pulling into a tighter knot, Beatrice's face falls. Shoulders fall. I feel my forehead wrinkle with hers. "What? I listen." But it's not said with Beatrice's usual pep.

Caleb sighs, so I match his frustration with a huff-puff of my own. "Beatrice. Not everyone is out to get you."

Beatrice chomps her gum like it's powering her whole body. I expect her to shout about that, the *out to get you* part. But Beatrice *surprises* me. *Surprises* feel like that time I snorfed a bunch of black pepper up my nose. "Why'd you turn the map like that?"

Caleb blinks. He was expecting her to shout at him too, and now he has snorfed black pepper. "Because it's easier to read when you point it in the direction you're facing, rather than reading it like a book."

Beatrice bounces on her toes, nods. "Okay. Okay." I feel her loosen. I'm amazed at how quickly she's untangling this knot. She's never backed off this quickly with Tessa.

And right when I think the name *Tessa*, Amelia grips Caleb's arm, points. Just ahead are Tessa and the four other adults, cresting the top of the bat bridge. They haven't seen us, I know, because I can feel Tessa's heavy coat of worry from here.

"We gotta go!" Beatrice says. We run downhill, toward a low white building, down a flight of stairs, and across a parking lot.

"Are you sure we can get to the trail from here?" Caleb huffs.

"Yeah. My mom works at that newspaper." Beatrice motions over her shoulder at the low white building we're passing.

We run over a dusty dry patch of ground toward the river, toward a chain-link fence. We turn left and suddenly we're under the bridge we crossed earlier. The smell of guano hangs in the air.

Caleb motions for the others to be silent, points up. They press their backs against the cool concrete posts of the bridge. Far above, I hear Tessa shout, "Luna! Amelia? Beatrice! Caleb!"

My heart twists like a rope toy. One bark and I could lead these adults right to my kids.

My kids. Earlier, they said I was their dog. They all agreed. They haven't agreed on much, but that? They all said yes to that. I am their dog.

A man's voice—Caleb's dad—shouts again. "My kid will *not* be returning to his sessions with you, Ms. Greene. In fact, I expect a full refund of our money to date. This is ludicrous."

No more Caleb?

That won't work. They have to be together. I know that. I feel it. They are becoming a pack. But they aren't yet—not quite. They are *almost*. And I know how frustrating and awful *almost* is. If Caleb disappears from the pack, it'll never happen.

"I cannot believe they are out roaming the streets of Austin with that mutt," Mr. Caleb's Dad says.

Tessa prickles like a cactus. "That dog is a better person than I am."

My heart wails. Maybe if I bark now, lead these kids back to their adults, Mr. Caleb's Dad will change his mind. Maybe it's not too late for that.

But here they are, my kids, backs pressed against cold concrete in the growing dark. Their hearts race like rabbits; their breath is short and shallow. They don't want to be found. I feel this stronger than anything I've felt from them. They don't want to be found.

I can't do it. I can't bark. I can't be the one that makes them found.

They are my duty. My quest. Barking—drawing attention to myself and away from them—that goes against all my training. My duty.

Something slithers over my paw, and I startle. Tuck in my feet. It's a lizard, scurrying leftrightleft, mumbling to herself *hothothot shadeshadeshade.* I restrain myself like I'm on a leash; it takes everything I have not to nip at it.

I think of the bird. Of instincts.

Bad dog, Luna!

I should bark. I shouldn't be here, so far outside of my routine. All this chaos, it's making me a bad dog. I am itchy uncomfortable. *Hothothot shadeshadeshade.*

The adult voices calling desperation into the sky above us fade.

"This way," Beatrice says, pointing to the small dot of orange sinking over the lake, painting the water red and pink. "West. Don't you think?"

Caleb nods. "This way. I think. And fast. We have one hour to get to Hector."

⋆ 16 ⋆

IN THE WIDE, WIDE, WIDE OPEN, WITH THUNDER

It's the fuzzy part of the day when the sky is orange on one side and purple on the other. The lights from the skyscrapers across the lake flicker on the water, and the surface becomes more like a mirror. Mirrors confuse me. It's me, but opposite.

To our left, large hotels line the lake. To our right, daisies pop through the tall grass between the dusty trail and the lake's edge like my Tessa's lace curtains. Rows of canoes and kayaks line the shore, colorful as candy. Humans swish paddles through the water, skimming their boats ashore after the show the bats performed for us. Humans jog by, huffing and puffing, their bodies singing with the joy of movement.

A yellow butterfly tumbles up and lights on my nose. I cross my eyes, trying to see it. It tickles, and it's dusty. It's flittery and *delightful*. Amelia giggles when I sneeze. I didn't mean to propel it away.

We walk, and soon, we approach a statue. A statue wearing a hat and a long coat, holding a guitar, holding time still. Amelia stops. Stares. Behind the statue stretches a long shadow. It's not caused by the sun, this shadow. It is made of metal. It is a part of this art.

Amelia the Shadow pauses. Runs her fingertips over the art-shadow's silhouette. This shadow, it's not the same shape as the statue standing in front of it. The man stands still, but the shadow behind him plays guitar. Makes music. Amelia understands this immediately.

Beatrice tilts her chin at the figure. "Stevie Ray Vaughan. My mom's a huge fan."

We pause here while Amelia is *awestruck*. *Awestruck* is a feeling a bit like getting zapped by a shock collar. But better, usually.

A row of turtles is soaking in the last bit of sun for the day, lined up on a log like mushrooms. I can't help myself; I edge closer and *sniiffff*. Turtles are so interesting, like a lizard carrying a stone home. One of the turtles blinks awake. "DOG!" he yells, and rolls sideways *splash* into the water. The others follow: "DOG!"

Splash. "DOG!" *Splash.* "DOG!" "DOG!" "DOG!" *Splash splash splash.*

I didn't mean to scare them. I didn't mean to shoo away that butterfly.

I didn't mean to hurt that bird.

I keep scaring all these things. Is that instinct too?

"This is the right way," Beatrice says. It's not a question, but somehow, it is.

Caleb nods. "I think so. Yes. We'd know for sure if we still had a map."

Beatrice scowls. "Dude. Why are you always so indecisive?"

Indecisive feels like not being sure if you want to go outside to pee, or if you want to stay inside in the dry warmth. It's a lot like duty versus instinct.

I look around. Ducks bob on the glassy river, then take off in a chorus of flappy wet honks. White storks tuck their long stick legs beneath them, unfurl their huge wings, and lift. The birds are all headed to the places where they curl up at night. I should be doing the same, at this color of the day. I yawn.

It's past your bedtime, isn't it? Sandpaper slinks up behind us.

Yes. I mean, NO. I add that second part because I don't wish to agree with this bothersome cat who keeps appearing out of nowhere. How does he do that?

Our protagonist grows weary, Sandpaper narrates. He winks, or maybe he blinks? That whole one-eye thing. *It adds to your Unlikely Hero mystique. IF you wind up the star of this tale, that is.*

I huff, roll my eyes. This cat is infuriating. I don't understand most of what he babbles on about. We—the five of us now, unfortunately—are near another bridge. Cars rumble overhead like thunder. And then *thunder* rumbles overhead like thunder.

Here's something: I HATE THUNDER. Always have. If I were at home right now, I'd crawl into my safe spot: in Tessa's closet, under a row of low-hanging clothes. And I'd whine and shiver until the storm passed. It's worked every time to keep me and Tessa safe.

But here I am, out in the wide, wide, wide open, with THUNDER. I swallow. Tuck my tail. Peer up at the ever-graying, ever-growing clouds. They skitter across the sky like lizards seeking shade. The storm isn't here but it's coming for us, I can smell it. How do I keep us safe here?

A storm brews on our Road of Trials, Sandpaper says, slinking between tall blades of grass. *Tempest-tossed—it's practically Shakespearean, this quest of ours!*

Hush, you. The thunder rumbles silent. For now.

Ah, he says, winking (blinking?). *And excellent*

125

timing: our next obstacle approaches. If I only had some popcorn to watch this plot point unfold.

I turn, and I run into the back of Caleb's legs. A man is waving at us from across a wide expanse of grass. He's running toward us.

"Kids! Hey, kids!"

"Uh-oh," Caleb mutters. "What do we do?"

Beatrice tightens, but before she has a chance to respond, the man is here. He's an adult. I know this because of his thick glasses and the stubble on his face and the ink on his skin. My kids smell as scared as thunder. We are scared, I realize, because today we are hiding from adults.

"Kids, you need a leash on that dog," the adult says. He points at a sign near the statue. It shows a tiny schnauzer dog trotting happily on a leash. That picture-dog doesn't look like me. Just like the last picture-dog, at the convenience store, didn't look like me. Why do no picture-dogs look like me? I shouldn't have to follow the rules if the picture doesn't look like me.

"Oh, that," Beatrice says calmly. She doesn't smell calm, so I'm surprised at how milky smooth her voice is. "Luna here is a therapy dog. She won't leave our side."

I won't, I promise the adult man.

The man smiles but shakes his head. Why do humans do that so often, say both yes and no at the same time? "No, kids. Listen. I'm a police officer and I'm telling you, you need a leash on that dog."

At those words, *police officer,* my kids all stiffen so fast it's like a zip of lightning inside a churning storm cloud. Sandpaper clucks in the grass behind the statue. He sounds like he's really enjoying this.

"If you're a police officer, where's your uniform?" Beatrice demands. Caleb shrinks, bites his lip.

"I'm off duty," the man says. His eyes narrow. "Where are your parents?"

"They're off duty."

The police officer laughs at Beatrice's reply. All this talk about being *off duty* has me panicked. Why would anyone wander intentionally from their duty?

"You do have a leash, don't you?" the officer says. "Because I'll need to call an on-duty officer if you don't. . . ."

I'm on duty here, I reply. That gets ignored.

"What's your name, sir?" Beatrice demands. "How do we know you're really a cop?" It's *bold. Bold* is pretending to be a bigger dog than you really are.

The officer grins. "Smart, kid. You should ask me that. Officer José Ramírez." He flashes a badge.

"That could be fake," Beatrice barks. Caleb stiffens.

His heart thrums like hummingbird wings. He is ever-so-slightly shaking his head *no* at Beatrice.

"You're right," Officer Ramírez says with a chopped chuckle. "It could be. But it's not."

Another lightning flash. Another cluck from Sandpaper. Infuriating cat.

Amelia quickly unties the flowery belt looped around her dress. She slips it through the ring on my collar, then raises her eyebrows at this adult man.

The man sighs. "Okay, that'll pass." He motions to the rest of the park. "Now go in there and find your parents, okay? It's getting dark."

"Yes, sir," Beatrice says. Her shoulders relax a bit.

The police officer man turns to leave. Beatrice whips toward the three of us, juts a finger at the orange horizon. "So. Zilker Park. That way."

The police offer stops. Turns toward us again. Caleb takes a step back.

Officer Ramírez narrows his eyes. "You guys aren't headed there now, are you? To Zilker? It's quite a ways on foot. You won't get there before dark."

"Oh, no, sir!" Beatrice sings. She was a small barking dog a moment ago, and now she's a pleasant singing bluebird. "We just wanted to know! For when we go there, you know, *in the future*."

"Mmmhmm," Ramírez breathes. He doesn't seem

convinced by bluebird Beatrice. His eyes dart over these three kids, scanning each of them, landing longest on Caleb. Caleb bites his lip so hard I smell blood. "That park is no place for kids your age after dark. Do *not* let me find you there, you hear?"

Beatrice slides between the officer and her other two friends, and I admire her protective stance. Her smile looks like the fake plastic flowers on the tables in the church basement. "We're fine, Officer. Thank you."

The officer sighs like only an adult can sigh. "Don't make me worry about you kids. Now go find your adults." He jogs back across the grass. My kids exhale like deflating balloons.

"What the heck did you do *that* for?" Caleb demands, shoving Beatrice's arm. The spark of fear he felt just moments ago is now a flame of anger.

Beatrice nods, then shakes her head. Yes and no. "I—I didn't think he could hear me."

"Oh, we can all *hear you*, Beatrice." Caleb stomps off. "Let's go." His words are knives. He is as jittery as a tumbling river. That adult man really shook him up. "I don't know why we stopped here in the first place."

At that, Amelia studies the ground.

Beatrice huffs, shrugs at Amelia, at me. She follows Caleb.

Sandpaper chortles, almost to himself: *Ah, the*

poetry! These kids, not knowing if they're headed in the right direction. It's almost too delicious, is it not? This quest practically writes itself, Protagonist. They certainly make my job as narrator of this tale much easier.

I realize Sandpaper is talking to me, but it's almost like he's using words to purposely confuse me, like a stick he's pretended to throw but has instead tucked behind his back. I hate that trick. So I ignore him.

Amelia stays put for another moment, just like the statue next to her. My whiskers twitch. It seems she's unsure. Does she want to go home? She is *hesitant*. *Hesitation* feels like a pause in the wind, that moment when the leaves stop swishing and all is silent.

"Come ON!" Caleb says over his shoulder. We feel angry. He's more angry now, for some reason, than he was when he got punched. More angry than when Beatrice tore up the map. He is a waterfall, pushing forward.

I tug a bit on my new leash, but the Shadow is planted near the statue-shadow. The one that plays behind the man that stands still.

Caleb stomps; Amelia stays.

And this is them, I realize. Amelia lives in the past. Rooted to one spot because it's easier than dealing with what's ahead. Caleb lives in the future. Moving fast because it's easier to ignore things when you're in motion. Sad is the past. Anxious is the future.

"What is WRONG WITH YOU?" Caleb shouts suddenly, grinding on his heel to face Amelia. These are vomit words: they surprise him as much as anyone, and as soon as they are out of his mouth, he wishes he could lap them back up. His eyes widen.

He hesitates, a pause in the wind.

"I—I'm sorry, Amelia. I didn't mean that. What I meant was . . ." His eyes glass over. Caleb *never* cries. Never. I can smell how salty upset he is from here, but I can't get to him to comfort him, because I'm leashed to the Shadow. Leashes are a real pain in the tush.

Beatrice loops her arm through his. "What you meant was, *are you coming?* Because we're leaving now, Amelia, and we want you to come too. And we are definitely, most certainly, headed in the right direction."

And then magic happens. Way off on the horizon, where the orange dot of sun has now tucked itself in for the night, four neon lights flicker on. They are clustered together like a constellation, low in the sky but bright as stars.

Amelia points. Beatrice and Caleb spin.

Caleb's shoulders drop. He beams. Beatrice jams a fist in the air and shouts, "Woohoo, wouldja look at that! The Zilker Park moonlight tower! This *is* the right way!"

Our Merry Band of Five receives their sign from the heavens! Sandpaper shivers with delight. *It is exactly the sign they need to continue this quest. And to be walking toward the light! Oh, the imagery here is truly delectable, Protagonist!*

Caleb walks back to Amelia, anxious to sad, and grabs Amelia's hand. "We want you to come, Amelia. We should go now. We've got"—Caleb flicks his wrist-collar toward his eyes, rolling Amelia's hand with his—"about fifty minutes to get there."

It's dark, and I can feel her worry: when a Shadow enters the shadows, she can't be seen anymore.

Amelia runs a light fingertip over this statue's playful shadow. She doesn't voice it, of course, but I know she's saying goodbye.

One nod of her braided head, one tug of my new leash, and Amelia walks forward, sad to anxious, toward the magic flickering constellation on the horizon.

★ 17 ★

BUYING THE MOON

Austin's moonlight towers," Caleb says as we crunch across the gravel toward the now-flickering constellation of lights. They are low, far. "They were installed in the late 1800s and called moonlight towers because they supposedly gave off as much light as a full moon. They are older than most streetlights."

Beatrice yawns *bigbigbig*. But it's a fake yawn— she's not tired. She's pretending to be *bored*. She sneaks a peek at Amelia. "How do you even know this stuff?"

"I'm working on my Eagle Scout badge," he replies. "Austin bought the towers from the city of Detroit. They put them all around the city because Austin had a serial killer called the Servant Girl Annihilator."

"What? Shut up! This story just got interesting, dude."

Amelia laughs. Fireflies are beginning to flash low and yellow between the trees, and my kids' joy pops and glows like those bugs.

We pass a man meditating. We pass under a pair of shoes dangling in a palm tree. We pass a baby in a stroller wearing one sock. We pass a man carrying a small dog in a backpack—*lazy!* We pass a woman belting out a gospel song: *"Glorious Moon!"*

"It's true," Caleb continues. "Well, kinda. This guy was killing all these young girls at night, so the city 'bought the moon.' That's what they called it—'buying the moon.' They said they were chasing away the darkness by having a full moon every night of the year. They actually thought they could hire fewer police officers if they bought these lights."

"Hmmm," Beatrice says. I can tell by her tone that she thinks this story is over, but Caleb is too excited to stop now. He crackles like static. Like an electric moon.

"But here's the thing. The early bulbs were carbon, and they glowed so bright they sounded like a swarm of angry bees when they turned on. They'd drop ash on the people below. And the light was . . . funky."

"Funky?" Beatrice asks, and I can tell she's interested even though she's still pretending she's not. Very

134

catlike, that Beatrice. "Funky how?"

"I think it was kinda blue or something? The light. Anyway, folks thought it was weird. Unnatural. They thought these moontowers would make crops grow too fast. And make hens lay too many eggs. And cause things like swarms of locusts to attack, like in the Bible."

"Check*mate*! That is crazy. People are dumb," Beatrice says.

Caleb chuckles. We walk toward the light. Their human shoes crunch in the gravel. My paws would prefer mud, but I don't complain. Amelia slips her belt back out of my collar, and I'm grateful for the freedom. Night soaks into the air.

Your humans are decent, I hear. Sandpaper. I see his big orange eye first, then the rest of him slides forward.

Decent. I smile. *That's pretty high praise for a cat. You might even call them "clean" or "suitable."*

Well, muzzle me. Sandpaper actually laughs.

Now, now, he purrs. *I withhold any further compliments until I see how they fare at the climax of our story. One can truly see character once they've traversed the Dark Night of the Soul.*

As usual, I don't understand what Sandpaper means, but I don't like the sound of it: dark night of the soul? I don't care for the dark. It's taking every bit of my gumption to stay out here now, with my kids, while thunder (THUNDER!) rumbles in the distance. But we're walking toward light.

And so we walk.

There are fewer humans on the trail now. In fact—I look around—there are none. No one but us. It makes me feel *uneasy. Uneasy* is that jumpy feeling you get when your haunches *twitch* and you jerk awake and you can't fall asleep. I scan. I sniff.

And . . . oh! OH. UGH.

I smell it before I see it. It's overpowering, this smell. A mix of blue-smelling chemicals and . . . human waste? The scent makes me dizzy.

"Oh snap, is that a port-a-john?" Beatrice asks. She suddenly hops toe to toe on her toothy boots. "Just in time. I gotta go, man!"

Beatrice runs to the tall box, swings open a flimsy plastic door, and lets it bang shut behind her. *Click!*

I am shoved backward by the smell that comes with the open and close of that door. My eyes water. I shiver. It is overpowering to my sensitive nostrils, this scent. And Beatrice has locked herself in there with it?! I paw at the corner of the door, *scritch scritch.*

Amelia pats my head, bends to pet Sandpaper. Sandpaper lets her. Purrs.

I present myself for petting now, Sandpaper

announces, *for we have reached the fun-and-games portion of our quest.*

Beatrice bursts forth from the plastic box in a cloud of blue stink and relief. "Whew, I feel better. Anyone else?"

Amelia shakes her head. And slowly, we all turn to Caleb.

He bites his bottom lip. Tugs at the neck of his bloody shirt. Shifts on his feet.

"I'll be fine," he squeaks.

"Dude, when you think about it," Beatrice says, adjusting the knot of pink hair on top of her head, "the whole wide world is a toilet. Just ask Luna."

HEY HEY HEY, I say, brow wrinkled. *Did you not see how selective I was earlier in that park? I am very precise when I poo, thank you.*

"What I'm saying is—you don't have to go in there if you don't want to. Pee anywhere," Beatrice says, waving both arms over her head. "We won't watch. Well, Amelia might."

At Amelia's scowl, Beatrice flattens her lips. "Kidding! I kid."

But Caleb hears none of this. He's shifting and biting and tugging at the hem of his shirt. "Everyone is always telling me, 'Get out of your comfort zone, Caleb!' And I'm all, '*Comfort zone?* There is one?'"

137

Beatrice laughs.

"But when you get out of your comfort zone, you push into somebody else's comfort zone. Nobody ever talks about that part, do they?"

I'm not sure if he's still talking about using this port-a-john or not. A whisker twitch tells me Beatrice is unsure too. "Dude," she says, "you don't have to do this."

"Oh, but I do!" Caleb bellows. "Don't you see? This is my Mount Everest! This is my white whale! This is my passing-the-driver's-test!" He jabs a finger skyward. "If I can do this, I can do ANYTHING!"

Beatrice breathes in deeply. I don't understand how; we are RIGHT NEXT TO THE WORST STINK IN THE UNIVERSE. "We seem to be spending too much time talking about this but not *doing* this."

Tell me about it, Sandpaper says, lifting off his front feet to nudge Amelia's hand for more pets. *This is one dragged-out plot point.*

"Go! Now!" Beatrice orders Caleb. She points at the door of the god-awful plastic box. Caleb looks from Beatrice to Amelia, lip in teeth. Amelia nods once, points at the door as well.

Caleb strides up to the box, sucks in a huge breath, holds it, and ducks inside.

Click!

Beatrice and Amelia crackle with laughter, but it's not cruel; there's a warm, jolly undertone to it, like jingle bells.

"It'd be terrible of us to shake the thing, wouldn't it?" Beatrice asks, gesturing at the port-a-john.

Amelia scowls. Nods.

"Okay, okay," Beatrice says, palms out. "Just checking that that was definitely a bad idea. My meter can be off on that kind of thing."

We wait.

Caleb is still inside.

It smells like all the human waste in Austin is inside that plastic box that bakes in the sun all day.

I hork.

"My grammy, she used to go to this place where they play chicken poop bingo," Beatrice says. It feels like she's pulled the thread of that thought from between the early stars. "The chickens would walk around on this big floor, and wherever they pooped—bingo! That's where you'd lay a chip." She pauses. "I don't know why I just thought of that."

A twitch of my whiskers tells me Beatrice's throat is closing; the tip of her nose is tingling. This is a feeling called *nostalgia*. It is grainy and tingly and a bit yellowed, like an old photograph. And she misses her grammy. I nudge her shin with the top of my head. She turns glassy eyes to me, crinkles her nose, winks.

"You die in there, dude?" she yells toward the port-a-john, blinking back her tears. "I hope not. They wouldn't find your corpse for a week in all that stink!"

Blam—bam!

Caleb kicks the door. It flings open and *whams* back closed.

He opens the door more slowly, steps out, and sucks in a deep, heaving breath, hands on knees.

Is he okay? We are WILD AS WOLVES out here. I rush to his side, sit.

He lifts his head. Grins.

"I did it. Take that, Moby Dick."

There is a moment that seems to swell before Beatrice and Amelia both explode with laughter. "Uh, dude, I'm not sure if you meant to make *that* joke right next to a port-a-john, but it was"—Beatrice touches her fingertips to her lips and kisses them, then blooms her fingers out like a flower—"perfection."

Caleb sizzles with a mixture of triumph and embarrassment. "What? Oh! No! What I meant was . . ." His voice falters. I worry that he's going to be upset with himself, but he collapses into laughter too. They laugh so long they suck in air, clutch their stomachs. Their joy sparkles like stars. Eventually, for Caleb, his snickers turn into shivers.

"Ugh. That was the most disgusting thing I've ever done. I wish I had my backpack."

Amelia rummages around in the tiny pouch strapped across her chest, pulls out a tube of goo. The goo that Caleb loves. He grabs it, smears it on his hands, all the way up to his elbows. "Ahhhhh. Why didn't you tell me you had this earlier?"

"Go on. Bathe in it," Beatrice says with a grin. "But quickly, dude. Clock's ticking. Hector won't be there all night."

"Now suddenly she's interested in the time?" Caleb jokes.

More yellow joy rises into the night like steam, and we're all delighting in its warmth. I wag. We are all okay. I am keeping my kids safe. This is my duty.

See? Sandpaper says. *Fun and games.* He nudges Amelia's hand. *Keep scratching the ears, kid. There you go.*

Up the hill, in a parking lot just above us, a car swerves. Screeches to a stop. Faces us.

We are blinded. We've been looking for light, and light found us.

Headlights.

★ 18 ★

PEBBLES FOR HEARTS

The rude smell of gasoline burns my nostrils. Two car doors slam—*blam! blam!*—and I squint through the purple air to see a car with triangle shapes painted on it. Mr. Red Hat and Mr. Dark Glasses slide down a steep, muddy hill to get to us. Red Hat trips and muddies his knees. A whisker twitch tells me Beatrice is mashing her lips, trying hard not to comment on that. Sandpaper disappears with a hiss.

"If it isn't those Meddling Kids," Dark Glasses says, and Red Hat snorts.

"What are you doing here?" Beatrice says. She—we—feel confusion, nervousness. That mix of feelings makes for one tight Knot.

Mr. Red Hat licks his teeth. "Y'all take my gas cap?"

Beatrice scrunches up her face too much. "*No.* What're you talking about?"

Caleb is silent. He's terrible at lying. Tessa always knew this.

Mr. Red Hat nods, then strains his neck side to side. It pops loudly, *crack crack,* like Beatrice's knuckles. "You owe me a gas cap. They're not expensive, but I'm not paying for a new one."

"We don't owe you jack," Beatrice says. The Knot is tightening: jaws, eyes, fists. "Run along now."

I feel Caleb shift behind me. "Look, I'm sure we can work someth—"

"NO!" Beatrice shouts over her shoulder at him. "These two don't get to march around being jerks and not ever answer for it, okay?"

"Jerks?" Red Hat spits to the side. "Okay." He takes a step closer to Beatrice. She does not take a step back, and this surprises Red Hat.

"Chill, both y'all," Dark Glasses says. To his friend he says, "They're kids, dude." Red Hat immediately drops his shoulders, but Beatrice does not listen to this guy. She is still tight.

"My dad is a cop," Beatrice spits suddenly, chin in the air. "Officer José Ramírez."

My head cocks. That was the name of the officer who told us we needed a leash. I don't think it was her father. A whisker twitch tells me Caleb and Amelia are both thinking this too.

Dark Glasses smirks. "Really." It's not a question.

"Go on, look him up. I'm telling you. You don't want to mess with us."

Dark Glasses has a toothpick in his mouth, and he shifts it to the opposite jaw. He ignores Beatrice's threat. "Right after y'all left that gas station, this group of, what, Luke? Five adults came up to us." Dark Glasses tilts his head, and I catch a flash of his eyes behind the shades. They are small and tight. "They showed us your pictures. Asked if we'd seen y'all."

The Knot tenses. The Shadow thins. The Waterfall's head rushes with noise.

"What did you tell them?" Caleb asks, his voice cracking.

Red Hat snorts at that. "Dude. We didn't rat you out, if that's what you're asking. But that was *before* we knew y'all stole my gas cap."

I can't grasp what these two guys feel. They seem numb to me. Dulled. And their hearts seem small, hard, like pebbles. It's like trying to read gravel. I don't trust people I can't read. My stomach tightens, ready to growl.

"But listen." Dark Glasses crosses his arms, leans against a tree. "They said they'd do anything— *anything*—to get information on you. We figure y'all are worth at least a gas cap."

Beatrice breathes out a word that makes Caleb blink.

Dark Glasses smirks, flicks a pointed finger between Amelia and me. "So y'all just load up your dog and your dumb friend here and we'll take you to Mommy and Daddy."

"Dumb?!" Beatrice's knots pull taut in all directions, fraying like a spray of fur in a dogfight. She steps farther forward, fists knotted.

Dark Glasses spits a brown stream of goo right next to Beatrice's boot, forcing her to step back again. "She doesn't talk. That's what they call those people. *Dumb.*"

That word, used like that, reeks like sour milk. Plus, Tessa would buzz as mad as a hornet at hearing his words, *those people*. She hums with fury when folks sort humans into *these* and *those*. Into *us* and *them*.

"I believe we all know who is dumb here."

I cringe at Caleb's cracking voice behind me. Red Hat—Luke—steps up to Caleb, and as tall as Caleb is, Luke is taller. "What did you say?"

Caleb flinches. I can smell how awful Luke's breath is from here.

Amelia's anger flares white-hot at being defined by these people she doesn't know. They did that to me too—made me feel *less.* How do some people do that? And why?

Amelia does what she did on the bridge. She screams at these two boys with the fury of a whole house burning: "AAAAAHHHHHHHHHHHHHH!"

Her face reddens, her fists ball. She screams until, my whiskers tell me, her lungs sizzle. "AAAAAAAAH-HHHHHHHHHHHH!"

Red Hat reaches in his pocket and pulls out a small metal thing. He flicks it open, then strikes his thumb across the top of it, *scritch.* A tiny flame bursts from it.

Red Hat thrusts the flame at Amelia, who immediately stops screaming and folds into herself. Deeper, deeper. A small, dark, tight shadow. She whimpers. Her eyes glass over.

My heart leaps into my throat and my every strand of fur stands on edge. My back arches. I growl.

"Just get in the car," Red Hat says through clenched teeth. The flame colors his face an evil orange, and the shadows leaping from below make him look like a skull.

"*Checkmate!*" Beatrice spits at them. She puffs, and the flame disappears. I can tell my humans' eyes struggle with this sudden darkness, but Caleb knows what to do. He pushes Dark Glasses Bryce, who falls backward over a tree root. Beatrice kicks Red Hat Luke in the shin, grabs Amelia's hand, and shouts, "Run!"

We run. But I flash my teeth at the pebble-hearted guys as I pass.

★ 19 ★

SHOULD'VE

They chase us for a bit, those two teens, but they quickly stop. Turn back. So we slow.

"Beatrice, stealing that gas cap was a stupid idea. I should've told you not to take it. Stupid, stupid, stupid!" Caleb pants. He kicks at a rock on the trail.

Each *stupid* makes Beatrice clench tighter. "You didn't even *see* me take it! You couldn't have stopped me."

"Exactly."

"Exactly."

They glare at each other so hard it feels like they're shoving each other. Amelia looks from Beatrice to Caleb and back again. I echo her feelings: both are right, and

148

both are wrong. They don't teach you about these tangles of thorny emotions in school. I don't know what my duty is here.

Beatrice is the first to speak. "I'm sick of the jerks always winning." She turns and walks.

So we walk.

Night presses down on us. Stars wink between the leafy trees, but I can't find the moon. Tessa likes to take me outside at night to show it to me. "That's what your name means, Luna. *Moon*." Over the course of many rainbow days, the moon changes shape. The moon can be a sliver, a strong claw across the night, like power. The moon can be wide and puffy, a chest swollen with held breath, like anticipation. The moon, when it's full, is the ever-softest pillow, its light a slow-drifting feather falling to earth.

I can't find the moon now. It unsettles me. *Unsettling* is a gray floaty feeling, fur and dust shaken off a favorite blanket. When a blanket like that is cleaned, it loses its scent, its story, its past. *Unsettling*.

Thank goodness for the moonlight tower. It pulls us like moths.

Caleb sneaks a peek at his wrist-collar. "Eight twenty . . ." he mutters.

We walk. We don't have flashlights or water or food, and it's not cold, but these kids of mine aren't dressed for a walk this far. We're dusty and sweaty. Green grumpiness begins to settle over us like fog.

I realize how thirsty I am. I pant, but I try not to let the kids see me breathing heavy. They don't need to worry about me. And I can't worry about my own needs. These kids. They're my duty.

Nearby: rustling. A stick breaks. Leaves crackle. My fur tingles, rises.

"Do you hear that?" Beatrice says, stopping short and grabbing Amelia's elbow. Amelia listens: more rustling.

"There's coyotes around here," Beatrice whispers toward the direction of the noise.

"There are not coyotes in Austin," Caleb says. But he stoops to pick up a sharp stick.

The rustling grows louder. I growl.

A pair of eyes!

I grumble. Sniff the air. Musky. Nutty.

Twittering whiskers poke out of the underbrush, followed by an adorably hooked tail. *Nutsnutsnutsnutsnuts* . . .

"A squirrel," Beatrice breathes. "I told y'all that was nothing to be worried about."

Night gets heavier. We carry it as we walk. The scent of pine needles sticks to us like sap. Crickets chirrup and owls hoot and the lake beside us gets inkier and wider.

"What's that?" Caleb asks, pointing several leaps ahead. Whatever it is, it's hard to see in the night. We get closer.

It's a fence, pulled across the trail. Our trail. Our path to light. With a sign.

I feel Beatrice untangling the letters of each word, fumbling like thick fingertips over tight shoelaces.

"'Danger. Trail Closed. Keep Out,'" Caleb reads.

We stand there stunned as shock collars.

A growl begins low and deep in Beatrice's throat. It rises. Escapes.

"ARRRGGHHHHH!" She balls her fists, grits her teeth, and kicks the fence with the toes of her thick black boots. The fence groans. "Stupid, stupid, stupid!"

She is echoing what Caleb said earlier. Tessa doesn't like when that word, *stupid*, is said in her counseling sessions. It makes her prickle. It's "unproductive," she says. I think that means it stops you from growing.

Beatrice is too frenzied for me to touch right now, but I move next to the fence where she can see me. I look at her with the most calming eyes I can muster. Beatrice stops kicking, drops to the ground, and sits with her back against the cold crisscross fence. But she throws her head back against it. "Ow!"

I sit next to her, and she tosses an arm over my neck.

"What do we do?" Caleb asks.

We go home, I answer.

But none of these kids say it. Why aren't they saying it?

The light of the moontower flickers through the wind-whipped leaves. It's closer now. Still far but closer. We are so close to Hector. So close to finding out about the whys and why nots of new friendships.

Caleb's heart ticks away the time we have to get there.

My whiskers twitch. These kids don't want to turn back, not when the moontower is so close they can almost feel its hum.

Melancholy. It's a feeling a little like being sleepy, but with some blue heaviness heaped on top. Amelia sighs, droops next to Beatrice. On the trail beside us, a tangle of star-shaped yellow flowers droops as well. They sunburned themselves all day, and now that the sun is gone, they're wilting.

A gate? An actual obstacle in the path. Sandpaper's voice purrs through the night. He swishes out of the tall, flower-spattered grass and weaves around Caleb's ankles. *Rarely does a metaphor present itself so literally.*

Caleb looks down at the cat weaving between his legs like it's the first time he's ever seen a cat. We are silent long enough for the purple night to notch closer to fully black.

"Huh," Caleb says, watching Sandpaper nudge his shins. "My mom always said I'm allergic to cats."

"You're not sneezing," Beatrice says.

"And not itching," Caleb says. Wistful. Wishful. He stoops and scratches Sandpaper behind the ear. Sandpaper's eye closes.

"All of this to see a crummy hoverboard," Caleb says. His voice is light, feathery like a tickle. He's teasing Beatrice.

She smiles in the dark. I can feel it. "Hector better be telling the truth. That thing better float."

Caleb leans forward, trying to see her face. I lean too. "Why does it matter? If it flies or not?"

Beatrice snaps up straight, eyes wide. "That's just it. He didn't say it *flies*. He said it *floats*. Floats! Lots of junk *flies*. But how many things *float*?"

We sit still, thinking of that word, *float*. I don't know what my kids are picturing or even if they are, but I imagine tennis balls and clouds and frisbees and bubbles. Nice things.

Nice things *float*.

I guess Beatrice needs to see something nice.

"Well," Caleb sighs at last. Looks at his wrist. "It's almost eight thirty. I guess we should—"

"Why are you in counseling?" Beatrice shoots at him. An arrow through the dark.

"Why are you?" Caleb shoots back. I'm oddly proud of him for shooting back.

Silence inhales, exhales. Silence is more silent at night.

Beatrice rolls her head against the whiny fence to look at Amelia. "I mean, I get why *you* are." She rolls it back forward, facing Caleb. "Actually, I get why you are too."

My whiskers twitch, and I expect to pick up white-hot anger from Amelia and Caleb. But instead, pops of yellow joy, like flashes of fireflies, poke holes through the night. Giggles?

Amelia laughs. Caleb laughs. And Beatrice, who I think was trying to stoke a fire, surrenders. She laughs too.

Joy floats. That's something else to add to that list. Joy.

They chuckle till they cry, these three kids of mine. As long as I live, I will never understand human tears. Humans cry at happy and sad and rage and bliss. Like feelings are one big circle, with tears gluing them all together.

Caleb inhales, exhales. "I have to testify in my parents' divorce hearing."

Beatrice picks up a fistful of fine gravel, lets it sift through her fingers. "That sucks." Amelia nods.

"Yeah. Well, *testify* isn't really accurate, I guess. At least that's what they tell me. I'll be 'chatting with a judge' about our 'family circumstances.'" When he says this, he wags his fingers up and down. He spits these words rather than says them.

"That sounds fun," Beatrice says, her voice as flat as cardboard.

"Yeah. And my dad's been telling me things to say about my mom, and my mom's been telling me things to say about my dad." Caleb tugs on the neck of his T-shirt. The blood there is dry now, and brown and crusty. I feel him missing his backpack, with its emergency water and change of clothes. Caleb is training to be an Eagle Scout. He is always prepared.

He is usually prepared. He was not prepared for this.

I'm so thirsty.

Caleb sighs. "It's all just one big game to them."

"Checkmate," Beatrice says.

"*Exactly*. Checkmate. And do you know how often a pawn betters the king in chess?" Caleb paces now, his feet squelching in mud. He cracks his knuckles.

Sandpaper follows, weaving around him. Caleb stops to avoid tripping over the cat, and stoops to pet him again. Caleb's pulse slows its rush when he does this. The Waterfall, softened by Sandpaper.

"You know what I'm going to miss the most?" Caleb continues. "Mom's family and Dad's family get along great. I mean, *great*. We do all our holidays together, all of us, and we sing and laugh and watch sports and tell stories. That's going to end, I guess. I won't miss the fighting. But I'll miss that."

We take a moment to think about missing things. I miss Tessa.

"You know what I should do? I should stand up to my parents," Caleb says. It looks like he's saying it to Sandpaper.

A noble decision, Sandpaper says.

"Yeah, like *that's* easy," Beatrice says. All three nod. They agree: not easy.

"You should tell them how you feel, though," Beatrice offers.

Caleb smirks. "Yeah. My dad doesn't really believe in 'feelings.'" He wags his fingers again when he says this.

How can you not believe in feelings? They are what makes life salty and sweet and chewy and crunchy and delicious and sometimes very hard.

Caleb cocks his head at Beatrice. "Were you crying in that weirdo museum earlier?"

Every part of Beatrice screams *no*, except for, oddly, her mouth. She chews the inside of her cheek. "I guess? I mean, yeah. But I don't know why, you know?"

Amelia nods fast at this.

"I mean," Beatrice says, shifting. Her arm is still draped over my shoulder, so the movement pulls me closer to her. "I do know. My grammy, she would've loved that place. I miss her. So much." Beatrice's throat tightens. I nudge her chin with the top of my head.

"My mom—she's more like a friend, you know? A good friend—my *best* friend, I guess. But not a mom. My grammy, though." Beatrice is fighting tears. I don't know why humans do that. Tears are wonderful.

"My grammy could do it all. Grandma. Mom. Dad. She was all of them." Beatrice sniffs loudly. Groans. "UGH. Sometimes I feel like I'm a balloon in a world full of pins."

Beatrice and I have this in common. I am soft in a world of sharp.

She continues, "Everyone else seems to be able to tell you exactly what they're feeling. *I'm happy! I'm sad! I'm lonely!*" She says these things high and yippy, like a squeaky toy. "I am all those things. All the time. All at once. I don't know how to pick them apart. It's

157

like trying to pick out one flame in a bonfire."

These kids are excellent at analogies, Sandpaper says. His head is cocked to the side and his one eye is closed thanks to the ear scritches Caleb gives him. *It truly helps me understand their human trials.*

At the words *flame* and *bonfire*, Amelia flinches. Beatrice must notice, because she leans toward her. "And that fire. It must've been pretty bad, huh?"

Amelia gulps and her throat is dry as dust. But she nods.

"Did anyone . . . die?" Beatrice asks. A whisker twitch tells me Caleb is about to tell Beatrice she shouldn't ask that, but Amelia quickly shakes her head no.

"Okay, good," Beatrice says. "I was worried about that."

I open my nostrils and sniff and it's true—Beatrice does have a whiff of worry about her. Worry smells like the stuffing ripped out of a favorite toy. Dry and messy. Easy to choke on.

"When did it happen?" Caleb asks quietly. He runs a hand over his head.

Amelia blinks. She's unused to being asked questions that require more than *yes* or *no*. She holds up four fingers.

"Four . . . months ago?" Beatrice guesses. Amelia nods.

"And what those guys said—that the fire department thinks someone started that fire. Is that true? It wasn't an accident or wiring or something?" Caleb bites his lip after asking this, like maybe he's pushed too far.

Amelia breathes in in in, and her exhale is shaky. I move between Beatrice and Amelia, lay my chin over her leg. She places her hand on my neck. She nods.

"Eesh. That is scary," Beatrice says. She places her hand on top of Amelia's and gives it a squeeze. I feel Amelia sigh, *Yes, it was. It IS.* But she holds on to Beatrice's hand, and it helps.

Beatrice leans even closer to Amelia. "Listen. You speak when you're ready, okay? Don't let guilt or pressure from anybody rush you. Parents want hurt to be OVER, you know? And I mean, I get it—who wants to see someone they love hurting? But you have to *feel* hurt to make it go away. That's the crappy thing about hurt. Well, that and it hurts."

Amelia nods. Swipes her cheek with the back of her hand.

"I never should've come up with this stupid idea," Beatrice says, and throws her head against the chain-link fence again. "Ow!" I lick her chin.

159

"You know what Tessa says." Caleb offers Beatrice his hand to stand up. "'*Should've* is putting pressure on your past self to do things differently!'"

Beatrice says the last part along with him. She takes his hand. He pulls, and she leaps to standing. Next he offers his hand to Amelia, who does the same.

Beatrice dusts herself off. "My favorite Tessaism is: 'It's only a problem if it's a problem.'"

Caleb singsongs the last part of that sentence along with Beatrice, and all three of my kids laugh. Their happiness together is like the whole of the sky and its endless wonders.

They stand awkwardly, limbs loose, their eyes trying to read one another. But I know the answer to their unasked question: *What do we do now?*

It is: *follow the light.*

Beatrice backs up, grins huge, sprints toward the fence, and leaps, gripping the chain link with her toes, her fingers. The metal rattles like tiny dull bells. She climbs. Throws one leg over, then the other. At the top, her shirt gets snagged on the pointy metal and rips. Just like when she climbed out of the church basement window earlier. When she reaches to loosen it, her arm scrapes the metal, and her skin rips too.

"*TTtttttsshhhh.*" Beatrice sucks air through her teeth. She feels hot-pink pain. "Check*mate*, that hurts."

She pushes backward, drops to the ground with a thud of her toothy boots.

I whine. Not just because Beatrice is now on the other side of the fence, hurt, but because *how will I ever get over?* I can't climb a fence! Is this where I have to leave them? I can't let a silly fence stop me from my duty!

"You okay?" Caleb asks from our side of the fence.

Beatrice examines the scrape. It's beading with blood. "I'll be okay. As long as my tetanus shots are up to date. Otherwise I guess I'll die a gruesome death."

She looks at us through the crisscross metal. "Okay. I guess, uh, Caleb, you climb with Luna, then drop her down to me. . . ."

This all sounds squirmy and dangerous and I whimper because there is talk of gruesome deaths.

But Caleb grins. Grins!

"Bea, anyone ever tell you that you make things more difficult than they need to be?"

Beatrice huffs. Her pink knot of hair slides around on top of her head. "All the time."

Caleb's grin grows. He pushes the fence. It's on wheels and it rolls easily to the edge of the trail. It wasn't connected to anything.

Beatrice narrows her eyes at us, then bursts apart with glee, like a balloon popping in this world of pins.

Lightning flashes with their laughter. I twitch with each flash.

We walk toward the moontower.

The sky feels heavier.

We *run* toward the moontower. Toward Hector and answers about friendship and things that float.

A cold needle stings my back. My neck. The top of my head. My back.

All faces turn up to the lightning laughter sky. It is no longer dotted with stars. It is now a sky of wrath.

It breaks open.

Sandpaper's eye clouds with disgust.

Rain.

★20★

LIGHT AS STEAM

Rain pelts us with hard, cold drops and it feels like getting hit with rocks. My kids hunch in half, duck under the leafy canopy of a massive magnolia tree. I follow. It helps. And the smell of the magnolias! The day-hot flowers steam and their scent is as warm and white and big as the sun itself.

The raindrops on the slick green leaves above us sound like hundreds of tiny drumbeats. A few stubborn drops worm their way through the leaves and find us, dripping cold on our backs, heads. I try to catch a few drops on my thirsty tongue. It leaves me wanting more water.

Rain! Rain washes away all the scents we've left

behind. That was the one thing I could count on—the scents to lead us back home. And now those scents are soaking into tree roots, washing into gutters. I cannot find my way back to the church after this rain. I pant and drool.

And I shudder. Beatrice shivers. Caleb appears to be calculating something inside his head. But Amelia! She sticks her cupped palm out from beneath the tree, watches the rain splash into it. She lights up.

She ducks her head out from this big green umbrella, tilts her face to the sky. Rain spatters her cheeks, reddening them. She crawls out from under the tree, her dress now soaked and muddy. Beatrice, Caleb, and I watch as Amelia stands in the middle of the trail, face-first into the storm.

Lightning flashes.

Amelia spins.

Slowly she spins, at first. Then faster. Then she hops and splashes in fast-forming puddles. She dances. The earth is steaming now too, the rain releasing all the heat the dirt absorbed today. Amelia dances in this mist. It smells musky, a large earth sigh.

Amelia ducks back under the leafy canopy and does the *come here* motion with both pointer fingers.

Beatrice beams. She crawls under the leaf line and

joins Amelia. They grasp both hands and leap and twirl in the cold rain. They jump in puddles, *splash*! I can't remember the last time I saw humans jump just for the joy of jumping. I had almost forgotten they can.

Thunder rumbles; the leaves continue to drum. My whiskers twitch. I expect Beatrice and Amelia to feel joy, but what they feel is . . . relief?

Release.

A sigh just like the earth.

I glance at Caleb. Surely he will have more sense than to go dance in the rain? Caleb has one hand on Sandpaper, who I didn't even know was under here and who is cussing like mad at getting wet. Cats know a lot of bad words and insults, it seems. Caleb shakes his head. But he's smiling.

"C'mon out, Caleb, the water's fine!" Beatrice shouts.

And he does it! Caleb, who up until four hours ago could barely leave his house without the strong-smelling goo that cleans his hands, crawls through mud, drags himself through muck, and dances on the trail with Beatrice and Amelia. Lightning flashes, burning images in my eyes of them dancing in the rain.

They are soaked: clothes, hair, faces. And one, maybe two, maybe three of them, cries. It's safe to cry while the rain soaks your skin. No one can tell. No one but me.

And they dance. And splash. And leap. And swipe at their salty eyes.

Rain is vile, Sandpaper says next to me, and I don't disagree. Thunder rumbles in my belly. *If I were the author of this tale, I would never include rain. It is an absolute abomination.*

But my spirit tugs toward my kids. *Look how much fun they're having!*

I can't take it any longer. I crawl on my belly under the magnolia leaves, and my underside gets gooey muddy wet. But I join my kids in the hard, cold rain, and I dance and splash with them.

I thought it would be miserable, getting this wet, this muddy. Tessa has always kept me neat and tidy, because I'm around so many people all day. But this? I feel *carefree*.

Carefree is an emotion that doesn't need me to study it. I am free of cares. Light as steam.

A sigh.

The rain stops as quickly as it started. When you're dancing in the rain, you can forget the cold. When you're standing in night air after the rain, the cold grips you to your bones.

We trudge toward the moontower light, now playing peekaboo with fast-moving gray clouds. We can't be far now. The lights of the tower are almost as high as the tops of the swishing pine trees.

Our feet are heavy, thick with mud. The smell is stuck in my nostrils. In my backyard, I like the smell, the feel of mud. Cool and musty. Here in the wild, mud is gluey and tiresome.

Beatrice shivers. Amelia looks pale and blue. Caleb wrings out his clothing, then tries to smooth the wrinkles he made doing so.

We are cold and wet to the core and muddy and hungry and thirsty and lost. I can say that, now that my scents have all washed away. *Lost.* Yes, we have light to follow. That doesn't mean we know where we are.

Lost is a stray dog, with no jangly tags to tell you where to return it.

"Hey, look here," Beatrice says. She runs her fingertips over a small board nailed to a tree. There are several small boards nailed to the tree, and a knotted rope looped over one of them. "A rope swing."

Caleb isn't paying attention. He's looking up at the moontower lights, biting his bottom lip. "Maybe half a mile," he mutters, then glances at his wrist-collar. "And twenty minutes to get there."

I whimper because by the time I look back to Beatrice, she's halfway up that tree with the knotted rope in her hand.

Caleb practically sizzles with anxiety. "What are you doing?!"

"Going for a swim," Beatrice says. "We're already soaked. And I've never been in Barton Springs before."

Amelia is already looping her bag over her head, dropping it at the base of the tree, and scrambling up the trunk behind Beatrice.

"This is *it*, Beatrice!" Caleb shouts. I feel—*we* feel—as bothered as a flock of honking geese. "I've finally hit my limit! I've followed you around all day. I left church for you. I used a port-a-john because of you. I danced in the rain with you—"

"You did those things for you, dude." Beatrice reaches the part of the tree where the boards stop. She throws her belly over a wide limb. I wince. I feel like I've been socked in the gut with her.

"I didn't even give you grief when you punched me. But *this*? Swimming in this nasty lake with snakes and fish and *gah*! Who knows what?! *At night!* No. I have to say no."

Beatrice stands. Wobbles on the tree limb. She clutches the rope. She is as high up as the roof of a small house.

Beatrice breathes in a deep, wavery breath. I can feel her jittery electric nerves from here. "You play enough chess to know, Caleb. You can't always predict the patterns of the other player."

And she *leaps*.

And she *sings*: "Fly me to the moooon!" as her fingertips sweep across the night, reaching for the light of the moontower.

Our hearts—my heart and Beatrice's heart—skip one beat, maybe two.

Beatrice sails, sails, sails out over the deep blue lake. And then, and *then*! She lets go.

She drops. Forever, she drops.

Splash!

Beatrice disappears in a ring of white foam. I whimper. *Where is she?*

I can't feel her spirit so far away, underneath all that water. I tumble down the steep hill to the edge of the lake and splash in its shallows, barking.

"Ahhhhh!" Beatrice surfaces, sucking in a huge breath. She lights up the surface of the water with her yellow joy. "Dude! This water is so much warmer than the rain."

The rope swings back to shore, and Amelia plucks it out of the air.

"Amelia," Caleb says. There is a twinge of pleading

169

on the edges of his voice. "Don't?"

Amelia smiles down at Caleb, and swings.

She lets go as gently as dandelion fluff and floats into the water.

I leap and splash and bark.

She surfaces, laughing. She splashes Beatrice in the face.

"Hey, you!"

They splash and squeal. I jump and bark.

"Come on in, Luna!" Beatrice calls. "Come!"

I want to go to them, I do. Their hearts, their voices call mine. They are my duty, those two. I whine. I rock back and forth on the muddy shore, trying to work up the courage to leap.

Courage. Before today, I would've said courage is a paved road, solid and steady and sure. Easy to map. But now I know courage is simply feeling *no* but saying *yes.* And we need it all the time.

I *leap.*

Water is everywhere—in my eyes, in my ears, in my mouth, in my . . . other places. The water is so warm I can't help but pee a little. I float to the top and use my big paws to galumph and splash and paddle toward my girls. My nostrils are *just* above the surface of the water.

I'm doing it! I'm swimming!

We three—Beatrice, Amelia, and I—splash around in the warm water. They swim and float and laugh and even though they can't see my tail, I'm laughing too.

We finally grow tired and swim to shore. Caleb is there, sitting on a wet patch of grass, Sandpaper purring in his lap. They are as content as a pink sunrise.

"That was fun but I'm glad you didn't come," Beatrice says, flicking her fingers and flinging water in Caleb's face. He smirks and wipes his eye. "The sooner you learn not to follow me into all things Beatrice, the better."

"I'm a fast learner," he says.

He is, Sandpaper agrees. *Knew immediately to scratch behind the ears.*

Amelia wrings out her dress, takes down her braids. Her hair is long and wavy. I think I hear Caleb gulp. Sandpaper must notice the shift in Caleb's attention because he nips the back of his hand. "Ow!"

Beatrice notices none of this. She's studying the rope swing.

"Hey, who do you think hung this rope here?"

Caleb blinks himself back to the here and now. "I dunno. I think this is a state park. Maybe someone who works here?"

Beatrice grips a knot and pulls. The tree limb far overhead creaks, sways. "It's strong. You think it's been here awhile, this rope?"

Caleb looks at it closer. "A few years, probably. Yeah."

Beatrice studies the rope. My whiskers tell me: she's *amazed*. *Amazed* that this rope is frayed and twisted and knotted, and still, here it is. A survivor, this rope.

Beatrice gives the rope one more mighty *yank* and the tree limb waves goodbye. "I like this place."

We scramble up the embankment. We're almost to the trail when, nearby, we hear rustling in the woods.

"Another squirrel," Caleb mutters, but he feels doubt. *Doubt* is the opposite of courage; you want to feel a *yes* but it is most definitely a *no*.

A stick breaks. A large one, by the sound of it. More rustling.

"Well, lookee here," a voice cuts through the dark. "If it isn't those Meddling Kids."

★ 21 ★

A LONELY LOST DOG
IS THE SADDEST ECHO

Dark Glasses Bryce and Red Hat Luke unfold out of the shadows.

They seem harder, meaner, pebblier than before. Red Hat Luke clenches his teeth so tight, his neck strains. He marches straight to me, scoops me off my feet. It feels like I leave my stomach behind on the trail, it happens so fast.

"Hey!" Beatrice says, but Dark Glasses Bryce slides between me and my kids. It's like a door slamming shut. I whine.

"We're taking the dog," Dark Glasses says. He shows them the palms of his hands. "You can either come with her, or we take her and turn her loose in some faraway part of the city. Hate for her to get lost like that."

LOST? I squirm, trying to wriggle free, but Luke is strong and he tightens his grip. We're lost now, but we're lost together. But lost *alone*? A lonely lost dog is the saddest echo.

"Put Luna down," Beatrice says calmly.

I wriggle more. Without even thinking about it, I bare my teeth. Growl.

I have an overwhelming desire to bite Red Hat's arm. I want to sink my sharp teeth into his flesh. I can practically taste it. . . .

No! That's instinct, I tell myself. *Choose duty.* I have been trained to never, ever bite a human.

My training did not cover this situation.

"So y'all just come with us, now—" Dark Glasses says.

"No," Beatrice says. She breathes deeply. She is not a tight knot. "It's not safe."

"We're just gonna take you back to your parents," Dark Glasses says.

Isn't that what I've been hoping for all along? Why am I fighting this?

Red Hat Luke begins climbing the hill up to a parking lot far above. His feet slip, and I squirm.

174

"Stay *still*," he mutters, squeezing me too tight. I choke.

I wriggle to look over his shoulder at my kids. Amelia paces, biting her lip. Beatrice breathes, shrinks. My eyes lock with Caleb's.

"ARRRRGHHH!" Caleb growls, kicking rocks up at Dark Glasses. "I am *so sick* of the jerks always winning!"

It's exactly what Beatrice said earlier.

And then, for a flash, I see it. At the moment:

Beatrice is the shadow.

Amelia is the waterfall.

Caleb is the knot.

It is the very beginnings of *empathy*, and it is beautiful.

The seeds were there for them the whole time, but now that they're a team—a *team!*—they know how to find those other things growing and blooming inside themselves.

Amelia blinks, takes a step forward, following Red Hat. *I'm not letting Luna get lost*. She doesn't say those words, but Caleb, Beatrice, and I all hear them.

My instinct: *Yes! They're coming with me!*

My duty: *No! They can't get in a car with these strangers!*

I have to break free.

I wriggle.

I push.

I growl.

I *hear* growling.

Growling that's . . . not mine?

Another stick breaks.

And then, between the trees above us, we see them.

Two yellow eyes.

⋆ 22 ⋆

THIS IS THE EXCEPTION

The growling is so low and rumbly I can't tell if it's coming from me or from him, Yellow Eyes. His breath is warm and stinks of eating dead things and garbage. *HUNGRY*, he grumbles.

He takes one step. Two. Out of the shadows now, into a faint circle of light. A patchy, wet coyote. Matted fur. One ripped ear. Ribs march down his sides.

HUNGRY.

He turns his yellow eyes onto each of my kids. Onto the two teens, one of them still holding me too tightly. We are all frozen under his gaze. Amelia whimpers. Dark Glasses Bryce cusses.

Red Hat Luke grits his teeth but mutters over his shoulder, "Bryce?"

Dark Glasses: "Yeah?"

"Follow my lead."

I feel Red Hat take a deep breath. Deeper. He readies himself. Shifts me in his grasp. I feel myself tense. He whispers, "One. Two. THREE!"

And he throws me.

At the coyote.

I flail through the air, paws churning, trying to right myself before I—

CRASH!

—land on top of a coyote.

It's like tussling with a bag of bones, trying to break free. He smells like rotten eggs and his fur is knotted, sticky. I feel a sharp scratch across my left hindquarter. I yelp.

"Luna!" Beatrice shouts.

Caleb picks up a stick. I can't see him, but I hear him whack trees near us. "Stop! Stop it!"

I wrestle free and leap away. We circle one another. We growl and show teeth.

I hear Red Hat and Dark Glasses slam car doors, start an engine above us. They ran, and my kids stayed.

My kids understand *duty*.

I growl louder. But this coyote is larger than me.

Hunched and fueled by hunger. Hunger is stronger than fear, which is what fuels me.

He tries to focus his cloudy eyes, and pity washes over me. *Pity* is the swamp water of all feelings: green and stagnant. Smelly. But I feel pity because this animal isn't supposed to be here, so close to a city. I feel it in his soul: he is lost. A sad, lonely echo.

But Yellow Eyes feels no pity for me. Lost or not, he still needs to eat. He flares his nostrils. Turns his cloudy eyes back on me. We begin circling one another, here on a hill covered in roots and rocks and slick leaves. My haunch burns where he scratched me. My back foot slips and Yellow Eyes lunges. Snaps teeth.

Hhhhhssssshhhhhh!

Sandpaper leaps between us, hissing. He lands, back arched, and swipes at the coyote's dry nose. The coyote wails, recoils.

What are you doing? I cry, scrambling back onto four paws. Yellow Eyes shakes off the scratch, hunches taller, growls louder. His nostrils twitch between me and Sandpaper, like he's deciding on a snack.

Every quest has a sacrificial lamb, Sandpaper hisses. *Or in our case, a sacrificial cat.*

As always, I don't understand this cat. But he's giving me enough time to flick my eyes around this scene to see how I can save my kids. My options don't look

179

good: scramble up a slick hill or back down into the river. The river, I guess? Can coyotes swim?

Take notes, Protagonist, Sandpaper jeers, never taking his gaze off Yellow Eyes. *This is the moment where the narrator injects himself into the story and emerges the hero.*

Wait! I shout. *You said the protagonist is the hero!*

Ah, you were listening, young protégé, Sandpaper says, back arched at Yellow Eyes. They circle one another. *But I said USUALLY, Protagonist. Usually. This is the exception.*

Sandpaper yowls like his soul is being ripped in two, and he leaps right at Yellow Eyes. *Into the Abyss!* he shouts, confounding as always. He is all claws and teeth and spit. Sandpaper bounds off the skull of Yellow Eyes and scrambles up the slick hill.

Come and get me, coyote! Leave these decent humans alone!

"No!" Caleb squeaks, but Beatrice grabs his arm and stops him from jumping into this quarrel.

Yellow Eyes roars with fury and scrambles up the hill, chasing Sandpaper. He loses his footing once or twice, hip bones jutting out. But he follows Sandpaper, up and away.

We, the four of us, are left breathless.

Four.

My heart whimpers.

I feel *forlorn*. It rhymes with *thorn* for a reason. It pierces. I hurt.

Caleb and Amelia both have tingly eyes, tight throats. Beatrice swallows, nods. She knocks on the nearest tree, hard. "He'll be okay. That cat? He's seen a lot. He'll be okay."

But she sounds *uncertain*. *Uncertain* feels swirly dizzy, like holding your breath too long.

Another yowl cuts through the night, and Caleb flinches.

Sandpaper. The hero of our quest. Just like he always said he'd be.

★ 23 ★

ONE STEP. TWO.

*G*rief. The hardest feeling of all to describe. I once stepped on a shard of glass, and it lodged in my paw for several rainbows before Tessa found it and helped. Before then, I couldn't stop licking it. It hurt, but I couldn't stop.

That's what grief feels like.

Fat tears shimmer on Amelia's cheeks. Caleb blinks repeatedly, clears his throat a lot. Beatrice scowls, sizzling with rage. We all grieve differently, which is part of the reason it's so hard to describe.

"Let's go," Beatrice says. She wants to go go go and forget. "We're so close. And we've got . . . what? Like ten minutes still. Before Hector leaves."

It's true too. The light from the moontower is so close, hovering almost over our shoulders. We find it, we find Hector.

The kids and I scramble up the hill, them pulling on tree limbs and roots to help get back to the trail. And we keep going. One step. Two.

That's grief too.

Soon, very soon, we hear a rush of noise, constant but gentle, like the earth exhaling. More steps. The exhaling grows louder, until it sounds more like the earth roaring.

A cool mist sprays us. We round a bend, and—

"Checkmate," Beatrice breathes. "This was why the trail was closed."

A waterfall roars down the hill to our left, washes over the trail, and plunges to the lake below. Caleb steps forward.

"It's a drainage ditch." He points to the concrete trench cradling this rush of water, ushering it into the lake. "This water isn't usually here. It's because of all that rain earlier."

Blasted rain! Why don't humans just turn that silly stuff *off* already?

Caleb takes another step forward, fingers outstretched. The mist stings them, my whiskers tell me. He squats at the edge of the water, dips his fingers in. He knows this waterfall. He is a waterfall himself, after all.

Chess is a game of precision. Water's game is chaos.

Caleb appears to be calculating if we can cross this rush of water. I feel fear growing in my belly and realize Beatrice and Amelia feel it in their bellies too.

I wish Sandpaper were here to overexplain this to me.

"Well, we had a good run," Beatrice says with an odd-sounding snicker.

Caleb stands, looks up to the top of the waterfall, down to where it crashes into the lake.

"Seriously, though." Beatrice gulps. "I think we—"

"We go." Caleb bites his lip, but his words are strong. "The tower is *right there*." He points, and I can even see the faint shadow his hand casts from the glow of the moontower. "We can cross this. It's five or six steps at the most. Worst-case scenario, we sweep into the lake like a waterslide. I think." He chuckles, but it has a cold sound, like clinking ice cubes.

I don't know what a waterslide is but it sounds alarming. *Sliding* is a loss of control.

Caleb places one tennis shoe into the rush of water, *sploosh*. Then another. He is wobbly, walking across, but his footing is helped by the concrete. His breath is high and tight, and I expect to sense fear radiating off him, but that's not what he feels at all. Instead he feels . . . exhilaration?

Caleb throws himself onto the other side of the waterfall. He beams. Spins back to face us. He's close but he feels far away. I whine.

"See? Easy-peasy. Except *ugh* wet socks. Glad I never have to do that again."

Beatrice and Amelia look at one another, and Amelia sweeps her hand over the water, *after you*.

Beatrice knots her flannel shirt high at her waist. "Here goes." She places her chunky black boot into the waterfall. "Check*mate*, this water is cold!"

She does it too. Wobbly steps but she makes it across. Now two of my kids are close but far. My whine grows higher, tighter.

"Luna, come!" Caleb says. "Amelia, follow behind her, okay?"

Amelia nods. I whimper.

"Come, Luna!" Beatrice says, patting her leg.

"Come!" Caleb says.

I dip one paw in the water. It's very different from the lake I swam in earlier. It's cold, icy, and it *pushes*, like water from the hosepipe. It's bossy water.

One step. Two. Just like grief.

It's hard to stand in water that's shoving me downhill with so much power. Amelia is right behind me, her skirt swirling in the current, and Beatrice and Caleb say, "Come!" So I keep trying. I am their dog. They are my duty. I whine louder, but the sound is swept away by the roar of the water around me.

I place a paw on something slick, metal.

My hurt back leg buckles. My paw slips between what feels like metal bars. It's trapped!

I yank and pull but I can't free my back leg. It's stuck.

Water is everywhere. It rushes around me, pushing me downhill. My trapped paw aches with the strain. I have to stand on tiptoe on my other back paw and hold my head up as high as I can to breathe.

"Luna!" Beatrice shouts.

I start scratching and struggling. I have made it this far and I am *not* giving up on these kids. *My* kids. My duty. My heart.

But my paw is trapped tight. My other paw slips.

The water rushes over and around my head. I choke, find my footing, and push my nose into the night sky.

"Her leg is caught in the grate!" Beatrice yells over the roar of the water.

"Bea, listen to me," Caleb says calmly. "Hold my ankles as tight as you can. When I yell *now*, you pull. Hard. Got it?"

My eyes flick in that direction. Beatrice nods once. She's listening.

Caleb shouts across the roar of water. "Amelia, when I say *now*, push Luna from that side, got it?"

Amelia must nod but I can't see her. I shift my weight on my one tiptoe paw. Breathe.

Caleb lays down in the mud, slides forward. He is coated in muck. "Got me, Bea?"

"I got you."

Caleb crawls into the roaring water, elbow by elbow. I feel the water shift to rush around him as he approaches. His hands wrap around my trapped leg, just above where my paw is stuck.

"Ready?" Caleb shouts. "One, two, three—NOW!"

Caleb sucks in a huge breath, ducks underwater, and YANKS. My leg twists and pain shoots through it. I try to yelp but I get a mouthful of water. I choke.

And right after that, I hear it, just as the water pushes over, under, around:

"LUNA!"

I don't know if humans feel this, but sometimes it's like time slows. Each moment around you feels longer, thicker, gluier.

That voice.

I've never heard it before.

It's as crisp as a church bell.

Amelia!

Amelia shovesshovesshoves and shouts my name. Caleb and Beatrice pull. We tumble and splash and crash and crawl.

We make it.

Me and Amelia and Caleb and Beatrice. We make it out of the waterfall.

I'm sucking in breath, lying in mud. We're all sucking in breath, lying in mud. We're on our backs in a pile of muck and wet about ten tumbles below the trail, chests heaving.

I didn't have to give in to the water like I thought I might.

Caleb is covered in wet leaves and mud and sticks. He mutters, "I'm sorry I'm sorry I'm sorry!" They stare at one another, eyes wide as night.

"We're all okay," Beatrice declares with a shiver. "We're all okay." Humans repeat things they need to believe.

But Amelia is crying. At first I think she's angry. She burns white-hot. Then I realize: it's pain. It can be hard to tell the difference between pain and anger; both burn white, because hurt is white. Pain is hurt in the body. Anger is hurt in the spirit.

Amelia blinks and blinks but the tears are still

there. Her ankle is twisted at an odd angle. It makes my stomach lurch. I think of my trapped paw. The pain was the same.

"Are you okay?" Beatrice and Caleb say almost on top of each other. They pause. Wait for her to answer.

She used her voice once, but she's not ready to use it more. Fat tears roll down her cheeks. She nods, sucks air over her teeth. That helps cool the white-hot a bit.

Beatrice and Caleb glance at each other. Did they really hear her speak?

"Luna?" They turn their attention to me, but I'm fine. My paw hurts and the scratch on my haunch burns but I stand and wag slowly to let them know I'm fine. Beatrice hugs my neck; Caleb scratches behind my ear. I pick my way over wet leaves and rocks and weeds to Amelia. She holds my face, stares deep into my eyes, like she's making sure I'm really still here.

I'm here. I don't know how much longer I could've stood on tiptoe on one leg to breathe.

They worked together—a team—to save me. The knot pulled. The waterfall dove into the rush headfirst. The shadow shouted and shoved.

I lick the tears off Amelia's face, like I've always done. Salty. Amelia is a rainbow, smiles through tears, and she hugs me.

Caleb, who is covered in sticks and muck and mud

for maybe the first time in his life, gags. He's watching me lick away Amelia's tears and he gags. "I'm sorry, Luna. You're great and all but *ugggghhh*. Face licking!" He gags again. Then grins. Winks. This makes Amelia laugh. If anything can outshine white-hot pain or anger, it's sunny yellow joy.

How do humans do it? How do they feel all these confusing emotions, all at once? All one giant spill of feeling. Exhausting!

"Here," Caleb says, helping Amelia stand. "C'mon."

Amelia drapes an arm over Beatrice's shoulder, and Caleb stoops so she can do the same with him. Gingerly, they hop her uphill. She sits on the trail when we reach it. I sit next to her. She hugs me tight. We are cold and wet and shivering and still flashing with white-hot pain, but this hug? It's perfect. How can hugs do that? Overcome all the other things? Like a whisper can be louder than a shout.

Amelia sits up suddenly, juts a finger at the moontower.

"Keep going?" Caleb says. He takes a sharp breath. "Oh, Amelia, I don't know. I guess . . . I could give you a piggyback ride the rest of the way. Do you really think . . . ?"

Amelia nods hard. She feels *determination*. It's what I felt when I heard her shout my name.

I did hear her shout my name, didn't I?

Beatrice, who had been pacing and cursing and cracking her knuckles and studying the moontower, stops short. "Uh, guys? About the tower."

We all pause. Look at her. The four bright lamps of the moontower blaze behind her, making her silhouette look small and dark.

"We have a problem."

★ 24 ★

FRIENDS DON'T LET YOU HOWL ALONE

Beatrice points at the four round, bright lights at the top of the moontower. Then slowly, she lowers her finger, directs our eyes to the iron tower itself. Then lower still, to the tall hill the tower rests upon. Down the hill. And to the lake.

The lake.

The moontower is on the opposite side of the lake.

"Checkmate," Caleb breathes.

"Yep."

We four look at the nearby moontower, now with an inky-black stretch of water snaking across our path.

Amelia blows out a long, shivering breath. Caleb bites his lip. Beatrice cracks her knuckles, paces.

"We could maybe swim it? We swam earlier. . . ." Beatrice's words fade away like the mist of the nearby waterfall. It's a big stretch of lake.

Caleb shakes his head. "No."

"I mean, I know Amelia is hurt. Amelia, do you think . . . ?" Beatrice's voice, which is usually as strong as a braid of thick rope, now sounds like a shoestring. She's trying to save our quest.

Amelia's eyebrows furrow deeply. She doesn't want to disappoint her friends.

Friends.

It occurs to me that this is what they are now, and I watched it happen. They are *friends.* I watched them bloom together.

Caleb shakes his head more. "No. It's not Amelia. It's me. I don't swim."

Beatrice cocks her head at Caleb, the top knot of her hair tilting as she does this. It's how she looks at her friend Caleb.

"You're studying to be an Eagle Scout and you don't know how to swim? That may be the most Caleb thing I ever heard."

It's funny, and I expect that to bring happiness to their faces, but it doesn't. They are all so mad. Sad. Disappointed. Upset. Thwarted.

"It's not that I *can't* swim. I *don't*. I don't like . . ."

Caleb pauses. Looks down at his chapped, raw hands. They seem to remind him of some other part of himself. "I don't like the feeling of water all around me. I don't like the feeling of my feet not touching the ground. I don't like holding my breath." He shivers.

Beatrice and Amelia and I all take a minute to realize: Caleb dove face-first into water to save me. And he doesn't swim.

Caleb steals a look at his watch. "It's ten after nine."

Slicing the day into seconds instead of shades.

We are *Almost*. *Almost* to the tower, but not there. *Almost* in time, but too late. *Almost* to Hector, but not reaching him. *Almost* to answers, but left with questions.

I led my kids to *almost*.

Goliath was right. *Almost* is as good as I'll ever be.

Almost washes around me, bowling me over just like that waterfall did. Along with running away from Tessa. Running away from my therapy dog pin. Hurting a bird. Crossing paths with dangerous humans. Sandpaper saving us from that rabid coyote. Sandpaper being the hero he said he'd be. Hunger and thirst and mud and blood and wet. Knots and shadows and waterfalls.

I look at the shine of the moontower. It's not a real moon. It's too bright, too electric. It's *almost*.

All the guilt and hunger and fury and frustration of the group overwhelms me, and I know I'm going to cry. Duty tells me to serve silently, to never draw attention to myself. But I need to cry. It is my instinct. I am giving in.

It starts low in my belly, but it grows. And escapes: *Hooow-Hooow-Hoooowwwwlllll!*

I howl at the moon. The almost moon. *Hooow-Hooow-Hoooowwwwlllll!*

I cry out all the feelings. *My* feelings. Not theirs. I'm so used to feeling the emotions of others, I could no longer recognize my own. My own guilt and hunger and fury and frustration. But these feelings are mine.

Hooow-Hooow-Hoooowwwwlllll!

And then my kids, my *friends*? They howl with me. Friends don't let you howl alone. We all howl at the moontower like wolves. Beatrice at first, and then Caleb. Even Amelia joins in. We four, we howl. *Hooow-Hooow-Hoooowwwwlllll!* Beatrice links her arm through Caleb's. Caleb throws his other arm over Amelia's shoulders. Amelia places her delicate fingertips on my head. We howl. *Hooow-Hooow-Hoooowwwwlllll!*

They do that confusing human thing where they laugh and cry at the same time. They smile with tears on their cheeks. Rainbows, each one of them. And they howl. *Hooow-Hooow-Hoooowwwwlllll!*

This howling, it somehow melts off a lot of the anger and aggravation. Mist from the waterfall. Light on the shadow. An untangling of knots. Letting it out helps. Tessa always said it would work and it does. We are a pack, howling together.

Hooow-Hooow-Hoooowwwwlllll!

The hill behind us rises into a flat parking lot. Car doors slam.

"Bea?"

"Amelia!"

"Caleb, son, is that you?"

"LUNA!"

★ 25 ★

THE DEBRIEFING
OF THE SHADOW

When you shine too bright a light on a shadow, it disappears. Tessa knows this. She knows that gentle candlelight makes a shadow dance, but lightning makes it vanish. So inside our trailer, Tessa has closed the thin lace curtains, dimmed the day. She even has fairy lights tucked inside gem-toned glass globes. It's warm and colorful here. It says *we're not angry but we need answers*.

Last night my pack of howlers were each taken to their own home, their own bed. Once I was dry and full of food, I slept, deep and dreamless. But Tessa asked them all to come back today. She has many questions. Questions crackle through the air inside the trailer like

197

lightning. But Tessa knows that candlelight works better than storms, so she's toned down the crackle to a flicker.

Tessa and Amelia settle into chairs. Tessa clears her throat. "Your parents were very nice to let me speak to you privately, Amelia. They didn't have to do that, you know."

Amelia nods. She feels a surge of sickly green guilt at the idea of her parents being mad at Tessa.

"But your parents said you were very responsive to their questions last night. You interacted with them more than they've seen you interact in a long time. So they let you return."

Amelia swallows. Nods.

"Whose idea was this, Amelia?" Tessa asks. She has notecards that have words printed on them, and I guess they say *Amelia* and *Beatrice* and *Caleb*.

Amelia points to one of the cards. Tessa raises an eyebrow. "Running away was your idea?" I can feel Tessa trying to imagine how Amelia, silent Amelia, could entice others to follow her far away, into the woods. Amelia smiles, nods.

"Did you ever feel unsafe?" Tessa asks. Amelia's head shakes, *no*. She looks at me, winks. I wink back. She did feel unsafe, at times. She doesn't wish to share that with Tessa.

"Would you do this again, Amelia? If this group were to continue?"

Amelia pauses. My whiskers tell me that *yes*, she'd absolutely do this again, but she feels she shouldn't say that. She shakes her head *no*. Tries to look sorry for what they did. But she doesn't feel sorry. She feels sneaky and brave, and she feels proud of her sneakiness and bravery. This I know.

"Amelia, I have to ask. Caleb told his parents that you guys were trying to meet up with Hector at Zilker Park based on an Instagram post he'd made. Is that right?"

Amelia shuffles in her chair. Nods.

Tessa turns on her blue screen, shows it to Amelia. "Was this the post?" On the screen, a tiny Hector poses with a piece of plastic next to a huge metal tower. Hector! I wag.

Amelia's jaw shifts. She nods again.

Tessa sighs. She reads something on the screen out loud. It's a language I don't fully know, but Tessa speaks it with some of her clients: "Voy a faltar la reunión mañana. Vida larga y próspera, pilotos. #badtothe drone #badtothedronepilotingclub"

Tessa looks over the top of her tiny glasses at Amelia, but Amelia doesn't shrink like a shadow sometimes does. "Amelia, you speak Spanish, don't you? Your abuela lives with you, and your father says she speaks Spanish at home."

Amelia smells *hesitant*. *Hesitant* is like a hiccup. She nods slightly.

"So you know that this post says that Hector *wouldn't* be at Zilker."

Amelia's eyes are on the floor. I expect to feel guilt with her, but I don't. Instead we feel . . . boldness? She grins ever so slightly at the worn carpet. She could've stopped their adventure, even without words. But Amelia needed adventure more than she needed routine. Shadows are easier to see when they're in motion. For one evening, Amelia was an in-front-of-you shadow.

And Tessa? She's not angry. If I'm not mistaken, she even feels a little proud.

"I can't guarantee this group will continue, Amelia," Tessa continues. "You guys made a terribly dangerous choice. Do you understand that?"

Amelia nods *yes*. And she means yes. That, she agrees with.

"Would you still want to be a part of this group, if it continues?"

Amelia nods, big and fast. She nods so emphatically the whole trailer bobs and nods too. *Yes!*

"Okay, Amelia. Thank you. You may join your parents outside."

200

Amelia wisps out of the trailer, and Tessa beams at me.

"Luna, did you see that? How well she communicated? Wow. I've never seen Amelia do that!"

I wag at Tessa's wonder. *If you only knew.*

★ 26 ★

THE DEBRIEFING
OF THE KNOT

So yeah, listen. It was my idea."

Beatrice's knees bounce, and the whole trailer bounces with them. "Am I in trouble?"

Tessa's eyes widen. Beatrice isn't demanding anything; she's asking a question. This is new to Tessa. "Should you be in trouble?"

"I mean, no." Beatrice grins like a cat. Glances side-eye at me. She totally thinks she should get in trouble. I cough.

"Why, Beatrice? Why run away?"

Beatrice stops bouncing and leans forward, elbows on knees. "We weren't running away, Ms. Tessa. We were running toward something."

She shakes her head. "That might sound stupid but it's the truth."

Tessa doesn't like the word *stupid*, so I'm as surprised as a pug in a pack of Pekingese when she says, "That doesn't sound stupid at all."

Here's the thing about knots: the things that weaken other items—water, weather, force—somehow only make knots stronger.

Beatrice and Tessa talk more. A long time. Tessa laughs and says, "Caleb? Used a *port-a-john*?" She makes a note on her notepad.

"I thought he might die," Beatrice says, but I know from a whisker twitch that she didn't really think this. This is a joke. *Hyperbole*, Sandpaper called it.

I miss Sandpaper.

"Did Amelia . . ." Tessa is itching like fleas to say *speak*, but instead she says, ". . . do anything special too?"

Beatrice glances at me, purses her lips. "Nope."

I don't know why Beatrice would keep Amelia's one word a secret. But she does.

"Were you scared?" Tessa asks at last.

"Naw," Beatrice says, and I feel like she means it. "We had Luna the whole time."

My soul sings and skips while Tessa writes something in her notebook. Beatrice cracks her knuckles. "But listen, Ms. Tessa. I have a question for you."

Tessa leans back in her chair. "Shoot."

"There at the end, when we were all howling? How did y'all find us so quickly?"

★ 27 ★

THE DEBRIEFING
OF THE WATERFALL

So you had a cell phone the whole time but never used it?"

Tessa looks up from her notes at Caleb.

"Yes, ma'am." Caleb cracks his knuckles. I smile with a flop of my tongue because he just did what Beatrice would do. "You won't tell the others?"

Tessa cocks her head. "Why wouldn't you want me to tell them that?"

There is a big sigh from Caleb, and I echo him because that's what good therapy dogs do. I hope I'm still a therapy dog. I hope I'm still a good dog.

"It was my safety net, you know? We were on this

205

big adventure, but I wanted to be practical about it. I knew you guys could follow us if I left my phone on, on silent." He pauses, then adds with a smile, "Plus I didn't want Amelia to throw it in the lake."

Tessa is surprised by that answer but tries not to show it. "Whose idea was it to leave?"

"Um. Mine."

Tessa sighs now too. Writes on her notepad. Here's the thing: Amelia gave the same answer when she was asked, *Whose idea was this?* And neither of them showed the signs of humans who are lying: sweating and shifty eyes and fidgeting. They feel they are telling the truth. And they are, in a way. They made the *choice* to go, to follow Beatrice. So it *was* their idea. That's all that matters. Not who led them out the window.

"You used a port-a-john, I hear."

Caleb fights a grin. "Beatrice told you that?"

Tessa shrugs, trying not to grin as well. "Did Beatrice do anything surprising?"

"Everything Beatrice does is surprising."

Tessa blasts with bliss at that. Caleb chuckles with her.

"How about Amelia?" Tessa really wants to hear news about Amelia, but Caleb just looks at me, then looks at the ceiling, as if he's trying to recall anything out of the ordinary. "No. I don't think so."

Amelia's one word—*LUNA!*—echoes through both our memories. But it stays there. Beatrice did this too. They're *protecting* their friend. Feeling *protective* of someone feels like offering them a blanket when they're cold. Beatrice and Caleb know Amelia's not ready for more pressure to speak.

"Your parents don't want you to return to this group, Caleb," Tessa says. "And that is of course their right to make that choice. How do you feel about that?"

Caleb is awash in feelings. Anger. Sadness. Irritation. Annoyance. He is a Waterfall, after all. Every emotion rushing in at once. But humans are drawn to waterfalls. They seek them out. Something about their quiet power, their crisp straightforwardness. Waterfalls are no-nonsense: water that falls. As pure as a poem.

"I didn't think they'd come look for me," Caleb says at last. "When we left, I didn't think they'd follow. But they did."

"They're angry with each other, Caleb," Tessa says. "But they love you. Love is stronger than anger. Stronger than everything, I think."

Caleb laces and unlaces his fingers. He feels *brave*, but it's a different shade of bravery than the bright purple boldness it takes to climb out a window and trek toward the moon. This color brave is airy and light, lilac, the shade of shadows fading and weight lifted off shoulders.

"I love my parents," he says. "And I respect them. But we have a lot of communicating to do."

★ 28 ★

EAGERNESS FEELS
BUBBLY LIKE SODA

Beatrice and Amelia squeeze down the narrow steps into the church basement at the same time, Beatrice leading, pulling Amelia's hand. Today Bea's hair is purple. "C'mon, A! You *know* this group session is going to be bananas. I can't wait to see what we do next!"

Amelia giggles dandelions. They sit next to each other. A handful of rainbow days have passed. My kids feel *excitement*. *Excitement* is what you feel when you dance in the nighttime rain with your friends, the scent of magnolia playing nearby.

I wag. The girls hug me.

"Hi, Luna!"

Amelia kisses me on the top knot of my head.

Beatrice bounces in her seat. "Is Caleb coming back, Ms. Tessa?"

Tessa paces the room. She is *unsure*. *Unsure* is what you feel when your feet sweep out from under you in a waterfall. "We'll see, Beatrice. I hope so."

Footsteps echo down the stairs. Beatrice hops up. Amelia screeches her metal chair on the concrete floor, *screeeee*.

A bike wheel.

Followed by a Hector.

Hector pushes his bike into the room with his right arm. Under his left is a mess of plywood, plastic, and wires.

Beatrice is stunned. "You! Where were you last week?"

Most humans would think Beatrice is being abrupt, pushy, but not Hector. He's a rock, after all. "I had a cold."

Amelia and Beatrice lock eyes, then erupt with laughter, like confetti. "A cold! Hoo boy!" Beatrice bends in half, hands on knees. I laugh with them with my floppy tongue, my waggy tail. I don't know why we're laughing at *a cold*, but it sounds like the opposite of *a hot*, so . . . ha?

"Is that the hoverboard?" Tessa asks Hector over their laughter. She points at the stuff he's carrying. It's a round board, a bit bigger than a car tire, with gobs of plastic and a long orange cord. He nods once.

Bea and Amelia are so busy laughing about Hector's cold they don't hear the next set of footsteps on the stairs.

Caleb stops at the bottom, beams at his friends. They don't see him or hear him; their backs are toward him and humans have awful forward-facing ears. Beatrice flings an arm over Hector's shoulders and tells him they looked for him last week. That they *really* want to see that hoverboard of his float. When Hector hears they were almost to the park near his house, his forehead wrinkles.

"You went all that way for me?" Hector asks.

"I went all that way for *me*," Beatrice says.

Caleb sneaks up behind them, stoops. "I went all that way for *her*," he says, pointing his thumb at Beatrice. Bea jumps, then throws her arms around Caleb's neck. "You're back!"

Caleb burns like a hot sidewalk but nods. "I'm back."

Amelia stands, smiles, squeezes his hand. Caleb might explode like a tiny sun from all this attention.

My friends, together again! And now we have Hector too! I wag so big my whole butt wags too.

Tessa is speechless, taking all this in. Her mouth is

open like a fish's. She doesn't yet know how well they howl together. Finally Hector says, "Tessa, can I finish the art project we started two weeks ago?"

"What? Oh. Don't you want to show us your hoverboard?"

He shrugs a single shoulder. "I'd rather finish what I started."

Beatrice beams at him. "I hear ya, kid."

Tessa smiles her wide, bright sunflower smile at her clients. "Then, yes! Great idea, Hector. Let's do that."

As she puts art supplies on the table and Hector stacks his hoverboard in a corner, Amelia tugs on Caleb's shirt, grabs Beatrice's hand, gathering them. I stick my snoot into their tight huddle.

Amelia takes a new screen out of the bag on her hip.

"Dude, your parents already bought you a new phone?" Beatrice says. "I need to try this whole no-talking thing."

"Definitely not your style," Caleb says, and all three chuckle.

Amelia swipes the screen a few times, then turns it toward us. It's a moving picture. A video.

"Is this drone footage?" Caleb asks, squinting at the screen. Amelia nods. Points to the words below the video.

"'I stayed late at the #badtothedrone meetup and

got footage of these two teens getting BUSTED!'" Caleb reads. "Busted?"

Beatrice leans closer. "Two teens?"

They watch. On Amelia's screen, Dark Glasses and Red Hat bang baseball bats on playground equipment, BAM BAM BAM. They shout, "Here, doggie-doggie!"

"Luke and Bryce!" Caleb hiss-whispers. "They were at Zilker!"

The fuzzy guys with pebbles for hearts. I feel my hackles rise.

"Tools," Beatrice whispers. I don't understand this because tools are useful and those fellas didn't seem useful at all. "They were still looking for us."

Amelia holds up a finger, *keep watching.*

A man—an adult—walks up to the teens. He's stocky, and it's hard to tell in this nighttime video, but he looks to be heavily tattooed. And he's wearing a uniform. A police uniform. Amelia raises her eyebrows.

"What the—?" Beatrice mutters, eyes on the screen. "Is that—*get out!*"

"Officer José Ramírez," Caleb says. Amelia laughs, nods big at this.

"The guy who told us to put a leash on Luna?" Beatrice asks. "The off-duty guy?"

"That same guy," Caleb says. "You know: your *dad*?"

They all smile slyly. They keep watching the tiny screen as the trio of guys yells at each other. The officer shouts things like "disturbing the peace" and "don't make me arrest you." Finally he leans in close to them and exaggerates sniffing them, their breath. I'm a pro at sniffing; I'd know sniffing like that anywhere. The sound on the video gets choppy, and there is a flash of two sets of metal bracelets before the video fizzles out.

"Handcuffs." Beatrice looks over her shoulder to see where Tessa is, but she is still lining up paints on tables, humming happily. "You don't think . . . that officer came to check on us, and he ran into those losers instead?"

Amelia nods big.

"That's exactly what I think," Caleb says, running a hand over his head.

Beatrice grins. "And hey. Dude *was* a cop. That's good."

Hector approaches the huddle, and my kids widen to welcome him. He glances at Amelia's screen.

"Is that Bad to the Drone's Instagram?"

Amelia nods, shows him the screen.

"It's a very fun club. Do you want to come next time? You don't have to have a drone. You can borrow one of mine."

Amelia beams at him, nods with *eagerness*. *Eagerness* feels bubbly like soda. Bubbly like gaining a new friend.

Caleb and Beatrice smile too. They are all *happy*, like fireflies lighting up a trail at night.

"Come on, y'all," Tessa calls. They sit. They art. Their happiness whirs like hummingbirds and they smile sunshine. They swoosh color and glue and glitter joy.

Pound pound pound. Snip snip snip. Fling fling fling.

I am *delighted* that my kids are together, and they are inside and safe. *Delighted* feels like a butterfly dusting your nose.

"Hey, wait," Caleb says, looking up from his pottery project. "Hector. Is that a one-eyed cat?"

Hector holds up the mosaic he's pieced together. "It is. This cat is everywhere. Follows me here every week. He's outside now."

"He's here?" Caleb, Amelia, Beatrice, and I scramble up the basement stairs, past the waiting parents, and out the back door. The adults rush to follow us, because us running out of places before has been troublesome.

Sandpaper!

He sits on the hot sidewalk, calmly licking his paw and dragging it over his head. *Greetings, Merry Band of Five. I'm pleased to be a part of the denouement.*

Amelia, Caleb, and Beatrice stoop to pet and scratch him.

You're still narrating, aren't you? I ask.

Ah, but our story isn't yet finished, is it? Our Transformation isn't fully complete. How goes the quest?

I think before I answer. *We never made it to the moontower. To Hector. We almost did, but we didn't. But look! Hector made it to us.* I motion over my shoulder to the pack member Sandpaper hasn't yet met.

Ah yes. Not knowing how close the truth is, we seek it far away.

Caleb scoops up Sandpaper, and it's like watching someone lift a bag of bones. He turns to his mother, who stands behind him on the sidewalk.

"Mom, we now own a cat," he says, and he marches back inside clutching Sandpaper.

Our eyes adjust from the bright Texas afternoon, and we follow Caleb and Sandpaper downstairs, into the drippy, odd basement once again.

"What are you going to name him?" Beatrice says, scratching Sandpaper's ear.

Caleb lifts him up, so they are eyes to eye. He twists and turns the scrawny orange cat. *Listen, new owner,*

Sandpaper says. *You are indeed a decent human and I am happy to have you feed me, but you can never truly OWN a cat, understand?*

I laugh. *Stubborn* is a cat, and that is that.

"Charles Wallace," Caleb says at last. "After the boy in *A Wrinkle in Time*. Because if anyone can time travel, it's this cat. You're right, Hector. He's everywhere!"

Caleb gently drops Sandpaper—*Charles Wallace*—so he can explore the church basement. As the cat sniffs an old radiator, I feel my throat get tight. My eyes get tingly.

I'm glad you're okay.

Sandpaper scoffs. *Is this the part where the awful mentor and the protagonist become friends? Right on time.*

Mentor? I ask. *I thought you were the narrator.*

I'm both! Keep up. Sandpaper glares at me. That one eye of his sure can shout.

I feel grateful all over again. *You were a real hero for us, you know? With that coyote? I wish . . . I wish I could've been that brave. I wish I had turned out to be the hero.*

Sandpaper sighs, drops into a crouch. He crosses his front paws, left over right. He looks wise, like a lion, except his hip bones jut out at odd angles. *Listen here,*

dog, and listen close. I'm about to give you a compli-
ment, and I don't do that for dogs very often. I don't
do that for ANYONE very often.

Before I can blink my surprise away, Sandpaper
continues. *A hero isn't usually a hero because of one*
big act of bravery. No. A hero more often looks like
a lot of small acts of friendship. Every day. Through
every THING. You are a hero because you never left
these kids, Luna. You never left their side. You never
forgot your duty.

THAT is a hero.

I'm all *mushy*, which is a feeling a lot like delicious,
juicy canned dog food. *Ah, Sandpaper*, I say, moving in for a sloppy kiss on his dirty, whiskery face. I
approach . . .

Whap!

. . . and get bapped on the nose with a warning paw.
Protagonists do not lick their mentors, dog.

A lot of laughter and chatter and paint splatter later,
Caleb looks up. "Oh! Hector! We forgot about the
hoverboard!"

"That's okay," he says, and he seems to mean it. "I
can bring it back next week."

Next week. Those words make Tessa glow. I glow
with her.

Caleb nods with *enthusiasm*. *Enthusiasm* is what you feel when you think something might float in your future. "Yes! I really want to see it."

Beatrice socks him in the arm lightly. "I get first ride, dude."

Hector blinks. "Only if you weigh—"

"—less than one hundred twenty-five pounds. Got it." Beatrice grins, and I'm not sure the others hear her sigh, "I'll *float*."

Nice things float.

Caleb stands, scoops up Sandpaper. *Charles Wallace*. It's a bookish name for a bookish cat, but he'll always be Sandpaper to me. As Caleb is bent over, Beatrice leaps forward and traps him in a loose head-lock.

"When's the court date?" she asks. "Amelia and I want to come."

Caleb straightens, forcing Beatrice to loosen her grip. "Does Amelia know this?" Their merriment ushers them up the stairs. Sandpaper looks as though none of this is surprising in the least. He leans over Caleb's shoulder.

Yes, yes. Excellent. This has all the makings of a fine sequel.

I should be used to Sandpaper tossing odd words at me by now, but I'm not. *A what?*

Sandpaper chortles, whiskers askew. *See you next week, Protagonist!*

Hector and his hoverboard and his bike clang up behind them. Amelia is last. She catches Tessa's eye from behind her artwork. She knocks one knuckle on the table, *look here*. And then she's gone too.

My heart feels empty without my friends. I'll see them in a few more rainbow days.

Tessa gasps. I rush to her side. She's holding Amelia's artwork, but it's more than swoops of color. It's letters. Words.

"'Test Beatrice for dyslexia,'" Tessa reads. Her eyes are immediately salty, her throat tight. "Yes! That's it. And from Amelia too!" Tessa clutches the artwork to her singing soul.

My friends each found themselves on that trail. Amelia found a playful shadow. Beatrice found a string of useful knots. And Caleb? Caleb who doesn't swim dove into the waterfall and won.

I've never been able to see the constellations that Tessa traces in the sky, her fingertip sketching from star to star. But I can feel, now, what those star-pictures mean. Amelia, Beatrice, Caleb. Me. Sandpaper. Hector too. Individual stars, but drawn together? We make something mighty.

Elated is what you feel when you're happier than

220

happy. So happy that you could leap off a rope swing and fly to the moon.

That's me. Luna. The moon. I was wrong before; the moon itself *never actually changes*. I am steady and true, and I never leave my friends' sides. But like the moon, *how* people see me changes. Sometimes they'll see me as a dog driven by instinct, not meaning to hurt a bird but oh. Hurting a bird. But sometimes they'll see me as their guide. Their light. My duty leading my heart. People see me how they need to see me. I am a therapy dog, pin or no pin.

I found the moon on that trail too.

★ 29 ★

ALMOST

I spend too much time in this leaky, flickering church basement these days. The very next set of rainbows later, during the high yellow hour of the day, Tessa and I return for a meeting of our Therapy Dogs Worldwide group. I'm still sore from the Big Moontower Adventure. *Tender. Tender* is a delicate, bruised feeling. Many folks think being tender shows weakness, but I know that it takes more strength to admit you need to heal than to bury your tenderness like a bone in the backyard. Bones in the backyard rot.

The room smells like dog breath and sounds like toenails clicking on cold tile. Very different from magnolia flowers and mud.

There she is! Goliath bellows, and I wonder yet again how a creature so small can make so much loud. The tiny chihuahua saunters up to me. Also how can a creature so small saunter?

Our Luna. I've been yanking my leash all morning to get here and find out: Did you do it? Did you qualify for your fifty-visit pin?

Every dog eye in the basement is on me. I feel like I'm being poked with dozens of broomsticks. And here's the thing: I don't know. I don't know if my Big Moontower Adventure caused me to lose all my therapy dog credits. Tessa should find out today, at this meeting, what happens to us next.

But that doesn't help me with these poking eyes. So I chuckle like Caleb and say, *I'm almost there.*

Almost.

There it is again.

Goliath and five other dogs laugh. At me. *Ah, Luna. Always at almost. Never fully there.*

But one dog isn't laughing. Samwise clears her throat. All ears prick toward her. *We are all almost, are we not? Still growing, I'd hope. We are all still becoming what we're meant to be.*

And then Samwise turns, leaving seven stunned dogs to watch her upturned tail (which means also watching her . . . *you know*) walk away. That dog really needs to meet Sandpaper.

Almost.

Almost isn't a feeling, but . . . it is. It feels *close* but not *there*. It feels like a fur coat full of static electricity or a too-short length of leash. It can feel like *frustration* if you let it.

Or *almost* can feel like excitement. Like you're on the edge of something wonderful, on the shore about to *leap* into warm water, to splash in yellow joy with your friends.

Almost. You still get warm standing next to a fire. You still get light standing next to a flame. That place next to wonderful? It's pretty great too.

Almost leaves room for the universe to work its magic.

Here's what I know, thanks to *almost*: I used to think I needed to fill the holes of my clients. But we all have holes; they make us unique and beautiful. Like Tessa's granny's lace curtains. My job isn't to fill holes. My job is to love my clients—my *friends*—holes and all.

Almost to the moontower was exactly where we needed to go. I don't know what would've happened if we'd actually reached the moon.

THE END

(Almost)

AUTHOR'S NOTE

Two of my previous books, *A Dog Like Daisy* and *Zeus, Dog of Chaos*, both focus on the amazing things service dogs can do. Daisy assists a veteran, helping him manage posttraumatic stress disorder (PTSD), and Zeus is a diabetic alert dog, helping a middle schooler manage Type I diabetes. In researching service dogs, I found a lot of information about therapy dogs as well. I knew I wanted to focus on those amazing animals next.

First, to clarify: Like trainer Barb says early in this story, emotional support animals and therapy animals have a lot in common. However, emotional support animals are trained to assist one person with his/her specific needs, and therapy animals are trained to assist a variety of people in a variety of scenarios.

Therapy pets are often found in hospitals, nursing homes, and retirement centers. They can also be found lending a paw in libraries and reading programs. Many therapy dogs assist counselors and therapists as they visit with their clients. I wanted to share the story of those calm and calming pets, the ones that assist counselors. After all, every one of us has struggled with defining and managing emotions at some point. Therapy dogs are trained to help us with that task.

Luna's network of fellow therapy dogs is based on the real-life Therapy Dogs International (www.tdi-dog .org/default.aspx), and the training she receives is based on the guidelines of the American Kennel Club (see www.akc.org/products-services/training-programs/ akc-therapy-dog-program for information pertaining to therapy dogs). Visit those two sites if you're interested in learning more about how to train your dog to become a therapy pet!

One thing to note: the guidelines for training a pet to become a therapy animal aren't standardized or consistent, so if you're interested in training a therapy pet, research first to pick a reputable organization near you.

I'm grateful to Dee Mathues and Missy Williams, both volunteers with a Nashville-based organization known as Therapy ARC (Animals Reaching Clients). Missy and her dog McCloud (a Newfoundland also known as Mac) visit hospitals, senior centers, and reading programs together. Missy loves watching how Mac brings clients out of their shell and encourages them to open up. You can learn more about Therapy ARC through their website, https://therapyarc.org. A portion of the sales of *Luna Howls at the Moon* will go to Therapy ARC.

My gratitude also goes to Sasha Cory-Pack. Sasha has participated in animal-assisted therapy since she was ten years old as a volunteer for the Red Cross, and I'm so grateful she shared her years of expertise with me. Sasha and her dog Percy counsel clients in the Nashville area (Sasha's kid clients named Percy after—you guessed it—Percy Jackson!). Sasha says Percy is excellent at gently pulling the emotion from her clients during their sessions. I saw Percy in action at a coffee house; Sasha, Percy, and I sat outside, and the number of people who approached our table asking to pet Percy was astounding. They stroked his fur, talked to us a bit, and left with a smile. Sasha says Percy does this consistently with her clients. "I believe [dogs] are an extension of us," Sasha told me. "I believe our consciousness and theirs blend."

I'm so grateful to friends Summer Curwen and Shirley Amitrano. Both of these women are counselors, and I'm thankful they helped me understand and develop Tessa's character and her counseling techniques. They also helped me shape Tessa's amazing clients: Amelia, Beatrice, Caleb, and Hector, and the challenges each of them faces. I'm grateful that Summer and Shirley took the time to help me better understand how each client grows and evolves in counseling. They both leaped at the chance to help with a book that centers therapy and counseling as positive and rewarding. I hope Luna and I have made you both proud! Please note that any errors made in this arena are fully mine.

My thanks to the city of Austin, Texas, for being so wonderfully weird. I've taken a few liberties here and there (placing a church too near the capitol building, for instance, and inserting a convenience store where I conveniently needed one). But most of these landmarks are accurately located and true. Visit Austin and see— you'll love it! (Plus it's full of tacos and music and boots and bats—what's not to love?!)

Dogs like Luna help us learn more about ourselves and our emotions. Those of us who love our pets know this instinctively, but many dogs work hard to help humans with a variety of feelings and tasks every day. Thank you to the trainers and animals who help humans navigate this world with a little more wag and a lot more drool. Not every superhero wears a cape; some of them wear dog collars.

ACKNOWLEDGMENTS

Thank you to the Kings and the Criscones for always cheering me on. I love y'all!

Thank you, Erica Rodgers, for being my first read and fast friend. I'm so grateful to be on this journey with you!

Thank you to the Society of Children's Book Writers and Illustrators (SCBWI), particularly the Midsouth chapter. You've given me skills and laughter and friendships to last a lifetime.

Thank you to Jeremy Cerveny, my Austin tour guide. I appreciate you showing me your stomping grounds!

Thank you to Josh Adams of Adams Literary. I feel so grateful that my agent is also my friend.

Thank you to Ben Rosenthal, my editor, who has now navigated three dog-worlds with me and who cheers on each story uniquely and with great grace. I'm grateful to all at Katherine Tegen Books for the beautiful stories they create for young readers.

A continued thank-you to all the booksellers, librarians, teachers, bloggers, festival organizers, parents, and grandparents who share books with kids! Luna would tell you: there is no better way to grow empathy than through a story.

A thank-you to my muses—Lucky (golden doodle), Cookie (cockapoo), Myrtle (pug), Nala (calico cat), and Daisy (mutt-cat). You make my life much messier and far more fun.

Thank you to the Tubbs, the Kites, the Grishams, the Goodmans, and the O'Donnells. I'm grateful to have such a large, beautiful, supportive family.

Thank you to Byron, Chloe, and Jack, always. There is no pack I'd rather howl with. I love you!

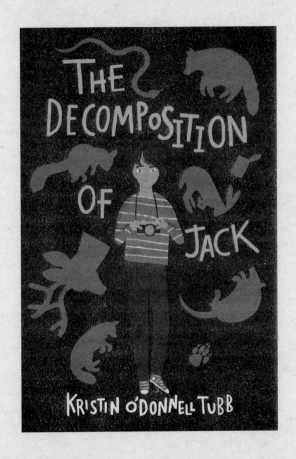

SCRAPE OR WAVE

When Mom offers me the option of scraping the roadkill off the highway or waving the cars around, I've learned to just suck it up and scrape. You get scowled at when you wave the cars around. You get honked at and swerved at. You get recognized.

But the scraping? You can keep your head down. And if it's cold, like today, you can tuck all but your eyes into your scarf. Sure, the folks in Abington likely know it's me out there with the snow shovel and bucket when they see my mom diverting traffic. But they can't look me in the eyes. I can't stand it when they look me in the eyes.

It's the pity. In their eyes. I don't like being pitied.

1

Because (a) I don't deserve it. They don't know the real story. And (b) who wants pity? Just the word is uncomfortable, like underwear stuck in someplace tight.

"Almost done, Jack?" Mom yells over her shoulder.

"Uh-huh," I answer through a pinched-off nose. This possum's been dead just a few hours. The bloat hasn't yet set in, and there's only a handful of flesh flies buzzing around.

The possum is heavier than I expect when I heft it off the pavement with the snow shovel. Much heavier. I'm guessing he had been maybe four years old, based on his size. Pretty rare.

I dump the possum into one of those huge paint buckets you get at the Home Depot. His body plunks into it with a crunching, smooshing sound. Bile rises in my throat. That noise gets me every time. Maggots, I can handle. Protruding bones, puddles of blood, strewn intestines—all okay. But the sound of the carcass echoing against the walls of a bucket, the stench of decay poofing up like a tiny green mushroom cloud—I still want to hurl.

"Easy, Jack!" Mom shouts. "You don't want to destroy its—"

HOOOOONNNNKKKK!

Mom's complaints about my roadkill undertaking skills are drowned out by another ticked-off motorist. I snap the lid onto the paint bucket.

But before we go: a roadside memorial fit for an old possum like this one. I scan the ditch next to the highway. There's a patch of dandelion pushing through a crack in the pavement as it tumbles down into the ditch. That dandelion is a survivor like this possum was. The flowers have turned to fluff and they're scraggly, patchy, which kinda reminds me of the rounded rump of this old fella. I pluck the weed and place it gently where the possum once was.

I always feel like I should say something profound in these moments, but I've never come up with anything that sounds right. Something to maybe usher these animals into the Big After. But it's hard to come up with something poetic when you don't know what After looks like. I shiver. "Sorry you had to go," I mumble at last.

I hoist the paint bucket and the shovel and head toward our beat-up station wagon.

The hatch of the wagon groans open. "Mom, there's nowhere to put this."

Mom waves away my hint that we leave this one behind. "Just shove some of the groceries aside."

I sigh and cram the bucket holding a dead possum inside our car, next to the ground beef, then join Mom in the front seat.

"What a score!" Mom says, blowing on her glove-less hands. She whips out her phone. I know she's logging on to iNaturalist.com and recording where and when—the exact spot, the exact time—we found our meaty little friend. I'll call him Gutsy. It's been a while since we've had a Gutsy.

Mom cranks the car. "I love this road! Chock full of specimens!" She bounces a little on the springy, wide car seat, and I can't help but smile. She's like a kid getting a present when she finds a fresh new hunk of animal carcass on the side of the road.

The Tennessee hills fly by while Mom rattles off her favorite finds from this stretch of highway. "Remember that small buck, Jack? Two points, I think. Wow. He was something else. Almost never got him home, ha! Thank goodness for bungee cords. Roof is still dented in. And the fox, remember? That red coat. Amazing. And, oh, the armadillos! Still can't get past the fact they've made their way over the—"

Mom slams on the brakes. I jerk forward against the seat belt. Mom's nostrils twitch. It makes me think of blowflies. Those little pests can smell death up to ten miles away.

Then, the smell hits me, too. There is no mistaking that smell.

"No, Mom," I say, shaking my head. "We can't put

that in our car. Plus, we already found one today. We don't need a—"

"Skunk!" Mom says. She puts the car into park and hops out before I can finish.

Mom is hunched over, her sparkly, excited eyes scanning left and right for the skunk. I see it, the pile of black-white-red fur ahead, but I don't point it out. Maybe she'll miss it. Maybe she'll—

"There!" she says, and bounces on her toes. "Scrape or wave, Jack?"

I crawl out of the car. Eesh—the skunk musk is so strong it makes my eyes water, even here, ten feet away. No way I'm scraping that mess up. Nope. I'll take my chances waving. I hand Mom the shovel.

"Chicken," she says with a wink.

"If it was a chicken, I'd scrape it."

Mom laughs, a sort of snort-giggle that makes me laugh, too.

She jogs over to the carcass and begins whistling. It's her trick for not breathing in through her nose. I haven't learned how to do it yet. I still dab a bit of Vicks VapoRub under my nose every time I have to peel a carcass off the road. It smells like being stabbed in the sinuses with ten thousand pine needles, but it mostly wipes out the stench.

I turn to face the oncoming traffic. My breath puffs

in the cold air, and I think about how each one of those puffs proves I'm alive. *Puff puff puff.* Molecules that were once a part of me, now in the air, fading away.

I wave two cars around. They swing wide, passing me, our swagger wagon, and Mom and her treasure. Questioning looks, but nothing mean. Maybe we can get out of here with relative ease. I turn to check on our progress.

"Whoo! This little stinker is a real prize, Jack!" my mom yells. "Young. Most of the entrails intact. And just wait till you see the gams on him!" I shake off a smile.

Beebeep! Beep!

The friendly little horn toot makes me jump.

"Everything okay, soldier?" The voice booms out of a tiny Lexus next to me. Soldier. He's referring to my camo pants.

"Yes, sir. We just—"

My voice stops working when I lean down to eye level with the car. There, in the passenger seat, is a pair of Algebra Green eyes. I call it that color—Algebra Green—because these particular eyes hang in the head that sits diagonally behind me in Algebra. The Algebra Green eyes, I avoid at all costs.

"You need to use my cell phone or something?" her dad asks. "Call a tow?"

I shake my head, but my stupid voice is still MIA.

My mom walks up just then, shows me the yellow bucket that reeks to high heaven. "Got him, Jack. Now, let's go eat lunch."

2

THE WORLD IN A 3 X 5 SQUARE

Screee-BLAM!

The screen door into the backyard bangs shut, but that doesn't bother the buzzards hanging out there one bit. They're used to it.

I walk right up to a gaggle of them—I don't know if they really are called a gaggle, but *gag* seems to fit— and stomp my foot. "Go on! Get outta here!"

Two of the greasy birds hop a few feet away and peck at another carcass. The third sizes me up with beady black eyes.

I'm not mad. He's just having a little snack. Doing what his bird-brain instincts tell him to do. He doesn't know he's eating Mom's experiments.

I sigh. "C'mon, dude. Get out of here." I lean in

close and whisper, "Don't make me call Mom. You know what she'll do." I drag my finger across my neck, "*Kkkk-kk-kkk,*" then point at the bird. "You'll be laying right there next to them, bub."

This is hyperbole, of course. Mom would never disrupt the natural cycle of decay. In fact, she'd be ticked that I'm chasing them off right now. But I'm betting these buzzards don't know that.

The buzzard pecks at the decomposing rabbit—Cottontail—one last time. He hooks a string of entrails with his beak. He lifts one mighty claw and slices the ligament from the carcass with a *snap*. The bird tosses back his head and swallows the string of meat down his gullet before flapping away.

André shouts from inside the house. "Are they gone?"

I smile. "Yep. No more big, scary birdies."

Screee-BLAM!

"Don't make fun. Those birds could peck an eye out."

"Yep. They do every day." I sweep my hand over our backyard, littered with picked-over animal carcasses and patches of dead brown grass.

André's face curls and his whole body convulses. "Sick. Meat-eating birds? An evolutionary step gone wrong, if you ask me."

I look up at the birds, now circling wide and low

9

overhead. There isn't much of a difference between me and them, as far as I can see. We both stay alive by scraping animal carcasses off the highway. But of course I don't say that.

I lift the bucket I'd hauled into the backyard. "Want to see him?"

André's eyes light up and he whips out his sketchpad. "He's big, you say?"

"And pretty intact."

"Cool."

"Drum roll, please."

André gives me a drum roll by smacking the palms of his hands on his legs.

"Introducing," I announce, "the Acosta family's newest pet, Gutsy!"

The possum lolls out of the bucket and lands on our lush grass, quivering like jelly. André swallows and jerks his head to the side.

"What's the matter?" A teasing tone sings through my voice. I smile.

"Whew," André says, lifting the collar of his shirt over his nose. "Another possum?"

"They're not exactly speed demons. We see these old guys a lot."

André shudders. "Guess I'll get started."

While I rope off the area around Gutsy the possum, André plops in the grass and starts sketching. The point of his pencil sweeps over the paper and leaves a thick mark here, a thin stroke there. Before I know it, I am looking at the beginning panels of his next *Zombie Zoo* comic.

I stand there, absorbing it, like I do every time I watch André create his comic. To bring something to life, instead of watching it fade into death? It's like watching a movie run backward to me.

But there is work to be done, so I tear myself away from André's zombies. I turn on our construction-grade tablet and pull up the roadkill database Mom designed. Might as well start with Cottontail. Or what's left of him.

Subject—Cottontail: male Eastern cottontail rabbit

Estimated age—9 months

Day—11

Date—November 6

Rainfall—1.2 centimeters

Sun exposure—very little

Current temperature—40 degrees F

Stage of decomposition—stage 3, active decay/black putrefaction

Insects present—blowfly and fly larvae, maggots, beetles, parasitoid wasps

Odors—strong (linger-in-your-nostrils after you've stepped away strong). Methane and ammonia.

Notes—bloat and beginning stages of discoloration—yellowy fur. Orifices no longer pink but rimmed with green and purple.

I pause, then add smiley face at the bottom: ☺. Mom could use more smiley faces in her day. The faces she usually sees are grimaces, faces showing the last-words shock of *Oh no, a car!*

Next row of the spreadsheet, next rotting body. Giggles, I call her. A raccoon. And back and forth through the yard, collecting stats and avoiding roped-off graveyards and piles of buzzard poop. A rat. Three frogs. Two snakes. Several possums. A deer. Six or seven squirrels. A polecat, all nine lives used up.

"I gotta dash," André shouts across the yard. He drops his sketchbook into a backpack. "Going to the Sugar Shack. Wanna go?"

I shake my head and cross the yard to him, weaving through the tiny roped-off areas containing bones and guts and poo. "Can't. More work to do."

"Ditch it. I really miss hanging out with you, man. All you do lately is work, work, work." He marches as he says this, like I'm in the army or something. The Splatoon Platoon. I laugh.

"Yeah, I can't. My mom really needs my help."

André nods, squints. The look he gives when I'm about to get one of his voices. "You're a good kid, kid," he says in his best New York accent. "One a da best."

"You just love me for my roadkill."

He punches me on the arm and changes to a fluttery, high-pitched voice. "And your buzzard-chasing skills. You have *ahhhhmazing* buzzard-chasing skills."

André bows and tips his Titans hat to the dozen bodies wasting away in my backyard. "Carry on, carrion!" He hops on his bike and coasts down the hill into town.

Not thirty seconds later, three more bikes zip by. "Hey, Roadkill Kid!" one of them yells. I know the voice coming from beneath that spiky black bike helmet. It's Cameron Totallyawful from my Earth Sciences class. (Totallyawful isn't his real last name, of course, but Totallyawful is definitely accurate.) As they pass, I hear Cameron say, "*That* dude's not going to the Sugar Shack. Guy's got a whole bunch of yummy guts cooking in his backyard. *Mmm-MMM!*"

His two cronies laugh. Is it bad that I chuckle when one of them hits a patch of gravel and his bike wheels skid wildly? He doesn't crash, but he squeals like a squirrel escaping an oncoming semi.

So they're headed to the Sugar Shack, too. Right. I've never been. Nobody there wants to watch the Roadkill Kid scarf down a double cheeseburger. Folks always seem surprised that I'm not a vegetarian. For the record, the only thing I cannot eat are gummy worms. *Ugh! Cannot* do it.

Cameron started calling me the Roadkill Kid when he spotted me scraping a groundhog off Highway 98 last month. This is never a role I wanted, of course. It's a role I inherited, thanks to my dad leaving. *Running away,* actually. But, hey, those animals squished on the side of the road didn't get what *they* wanted either, so I don't complain. And at least Mom has one strict rule when it comes to collecting carrion—absolutely no pets. No dogs, no cats, no domesticated rabbits—nothing that would live inside a home. They mess up the data, but also, it's easier when you're dealing with a mole with no name. Until I name her Princess Elsa.

Just as I finish up my notes, I see something move out of the corner of my eye. Things that move are studied in my backyard, because they're a part of the decomposition cycle Mom's so interested in. It was just a flash, a zip through the tall grass, over the fence, into the trees. I don't really want to study whatever this thing is right now—*Super Smash Brothers* isn't going to play itself. I run my fingers along the chain-link fence as I walk the perimeter of the yard—*tingingingininging*—a warning to the thing that moves.

Whatever I saw is gone. But it was something, because there, in a patch of mud, is a huge paw print, at least four inches across. It is smooth and curvy and deeper in the front, like the moving thing pushed off from this spot in a leap.

And it is warm. That surprises me, for some reason. My fingers flutter just over the paw print, over the hollows in the mud. I don't want to touch it. This is movement, frozen.

I need to keep it that way. Preserve it. I consider digging it up, like a slab of rock containing a fossil, but I know that once the mud dries, the slab will crumble.

The heat is leaving the paw print quickly, like a ghost. And once the clouds break open and dump cold rain, I will lose the paw forever. I dash into the house and grab Dad's old camera. I blow on it once, twice to get rid of the dust, run back outside, and snap a photo.

This is going to sound crazy—even crazier than a kid who helps his mom scrape and study roadkill—but the sun is setting just as I snap the photo, and the crystals in the mud sparkle just so, and the curves of the paw soak in shadows like tiny, dark crescent moons, and the grass bows and prays around the edges of the photo, blurry and waving, and the whole picture looks like magic.

Mom comes to the screen door. "What's all the hubbub? One of Ms. Zachary's dogs try to dig under again?"

I look at the viewer on the back of the camera until

it fades. If I show this to Mom, she'll find a way to turn it into an experiment. I don't want to analyze this creature's every meal, every pile of dung. This animal is stealthy and sly, and she goes unnoticed, mostly. I know how that feels.

No, I want the magic a little longer.

"Nothing," I say. My stomach twists, a feeling I'm not used to since my stomach is made of steel. "Just some interesting maggots."

Mom smiles. "Every maggot is interesting! The recyclers of the universe, those little guys! Long live maggots!" She laughs at her joke—maggots only live about eight days—flips her dishtowel, and marches into the house.

I bring the picture back up on the screen. Amazing, even though it's just mud and grass and an animal print. There is something satisfying about whittling the world down to one three by five square. I brought this photo to life, like André does with his comics. A thrill shoots through me, like the feeling of jumping off a swing at its highest point.

I place the toe of my Converse over the paw print and squish, burying the print under sneaker tread. Just in case the rain doesn't erase it all the way.

"Come back tomorrow," I whisper into the trees. "She won't be here then."